"It's so beautiful,"

Jeri whispered, as she reverently set down the small jar filled with gold and picked up the stack of letters.

Wade's thoughts of her greedy motives were hastily pushed aside as he watched. He was fascinated by her, by the glow in her eyes as she touched her father's letters. She broke his train of thought when she suddenly looked up.

"I'm truly sorry to inconvenience you, Mr. Evans, but I'm not going into town. I'm staying here, in my father's room."

Wade froze. "Lady, that just isn't a very smart idea."

"Smart or not, Mr. Evans, I'm staying. I understand that you have several properties in the valley. All I have is half of this one, and I'm staying."

They stared at each other, eyes testing, probing, searching for weakness . . . or strength.

Finally Wade took a long, slow breath. "One of us is liable to be real sorry about that decision."

"Is that a threat, Mr. Evans?"

"No, ma'am. It's a warning."

Dear Reader,

Welcome to Silhouette—experience the magic of the wonderful world where two people fall in love. Meet heroines who will make you cheer for their happiness, and heroes (be they the boy next door or a handsome, mysterious stranger) who will win your heart. Silhouette Romance reflects the magic of love—sweeping you away with books that will make you laugh and cry, heartwarming, poignant stories that will move you time and time again.

In the coming months we're publishing romances by many of your all-time favorites, such as Diana Palmer, Brittany Young, Sondra Stanford and Annette Broadrick. Your response to these authors and our other Silhouette Romance authors has served as a touchstone for us, and we're pleased to bring you more books with Silhouette's distinctive medley of charm, wit and—above all—*romance*.

I hope you enjoy this book and the many stories to come. Experience the magic!

Sincerely,

Tara Hughes
Senior Editor
Silhouette Books

DIANA WHITNEY

O'Brian's Daughter

Published by Silhouette Books New York
America's Publisher of Contemporary Romance

To my husband, Carl,
who encouraged me to follow my dream,
then gave me the opportunity to do so

SILHOUETTE BOOKS
300 E. 42nd St., New York, N.Y. 10017

Books by Diana Whitney

Silhouette Special Edition
Cast a Tall Shadow #508

Silhouette Romance
O'Brian's Daughter #673

DIANA WHITNEY

says she loves "fat babies and warm puppies, mountain streams and Southern California sunshine, camping, hiking and gold prospecting. Not to mention strong, romantic heroes!" She married her own real-life hero fifteen years ago. With his encouragement, she left her longtime career as a municipal finance director and pursued the dream that had haunted her since childhood—writing. To Diana, writing is a joy, the ultimate satisfaction. Reading, too, is her passion, from spine-chilling thrillers to sweeping sagas, but nothing can compare to the magic and wonder of romance.

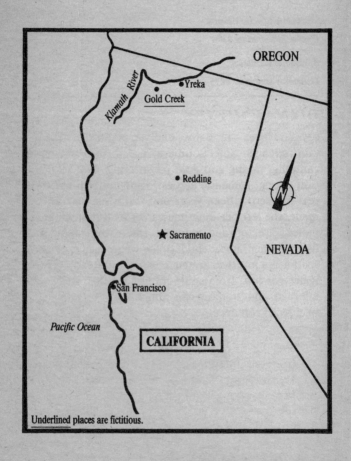

OREGON

Klamath River

● Yreka

Gold Creek

● Redding

N

★ Sacramento

NEVADA

●San Francisco

Pacific Ocean

CALIFORNIA

Underlined places are fictitious.

Chapter One

"Dammit, Murphy. Shut up."

The exuberant yelping stopped, and the yellow Labrador looked up quizzically. Wade Evans glared first at the dog, then at the chaotic mass of parts strewed across his cluttered outdoor worktable.

"I've got enough problems trying to turn this mess back into a working generator without listening to you excite yourself over every squirrel and coon in the woods." With a disgusted sigh, Wade dropped a sheared piston rod onto the plank table. He stared down at it glumly and speared his fingers through his already disheveled brown hair. "Looks like oil lamps again tonight, boy."

Murphy responded with a joyful yip and slicing swish of tail, his muzzle split in a panting, tongue-lolling grin. Leaping forward, Murphy bowed low on his forepaws, rear elevated and tail circling wildly.

Wade smiled, bending to give the dog's head an affectionate scratch. "Thirty-five in dog years and still acting like a pup. What's your secret, Murphy? Got yourself a lady-friend?''

Murphy looked incredibly pleased with himself.

"So that's it, is it?" Wade pulled up a splintered wooden crate and sat, straddling it with lean, denim-clad legs. "Guess I'll have to muddle through middle age by myself. Haven't met a woman yet who was worth the trouble she caused."

With his back resting against the cabin's rough-hewed sideboards, Wade surveyed the land. Stands of fir and pine seemed to thrust from the earth like huge green sentries patrolling the perimeter of Gold Creek Meadow. Butting against a heavily wooded knoll, the cabin sat at the south edge of the meadow. Beyond that knoll rushed the bright, clear water of Gold Creek, feverishly leaping over moss-covered rocks to rest momentarily in deep, cold pools before continuing its frenzied journey to the Klamath River.

Yes, this was prime land. One hundred sixty acres of meadow, creek, timber and wilderness nestled on three sides by Northern California's Klamath National Forest. It was some of the most beautiful in the Klamath Valley, and Wade knew those city developers craved it.

At the thought of bulldozers ravaging these virgin hills, Wade's eyes narrowed, darkening to the blue-green color of tarnished copper. They would turn this valley into suburbia, he thought, spread asphalt across the mountains, pollute the creeks and turn the Klamath River itself into a putrid, boiling sewer.

Murphy's sharp bark drew Wade's attention. He followed the dog's steady gaze toward the dirt road that wound through the forest to the main highway. Wade heard nothing, but obviously Murphy did.

"Something interesting, boy? Go on. Chase it off and teach it some manners." With an excited yelp Murphy bounded forward and disappeared.

Thin white clouds threaded hazily across the sky, criss-crossing the crystalline blue like stretched strands of fuzzy cotton. Wade watched them, oblivious to the passing minutes, enjoying the tranquil beauty of this fragile land. He finally stood, reluctantly returning to the worktable, refocusing his mind on the useless piston rod.

He glanced at his watch. It was nearly three-thirty. He might be able to get into Yreka by five and have Sid take a look at the rod. Sid's tool-and-die shop was the only place north of Redding that might be able to mill a replacement. Wade knew it would take a few days for Sid to complete the work, and he made a mental note to pick up some more lamp oil.

"Who are you?" asked a distinctly annoyed, feminine voice.

Startled, Wade dropped the steel rod. It fell noisily to the table, sending bolts skittering over the edge. He looked over at a young woman standing rigid and indignant, tawny eyes glinting as though he, not she, was the uninvited intruder. Murphy sat next to her panting happily, oblivious to any displeasure displayed by his guest or master.

"I said, who are you? And what are you doing on my property?"

Wade stared in disbelief. "*Your* property?"

Her curt nod was emphasized by the bounce of short dark curls which framed a determined face. "That's what I said. My name is Jeri O'Brian." She squinted up at Wade. "Now, who are *you*?"

Wade felt as though he had been kicked in the stomach. Jerome O'Brian's kid. Good grief, why now? After all these months, why did she have to show up now? His mouth thinned, dark eyebrows knitting into a single furry gash as he stared back at her. She met his gaze, calmly awaiting an answer, seeming unperturbed by his dark scowl.

"The name's Evans. Wade Evans."

He watched her face pale at his name, satisfied that she knew exactly who he was. Jeri stared at Wade intently, scrutinizing him with such thoroughness that he felt like a prize steer at auction. Returning the inspection, Wade allowed his gaze to travel pointedly over her slender frame. A white knit cropped top, clinging damply in the muggy July heat, contoured small well rounded breasts, and snug jeans outlined the sleek curve of hip and thigh. Tiny feet, spread slightly and planted resolutely in the soft dirt, were dusty and shoeless.

Slip of a girl, but well packaged, Wade decided.

"I thought you'd be older," she said.

Wade bent slowly, scooping bolts from the ground with one sweep of his big hand and dropping them casually on the table. He straightened and met her direct stare. "I thought you'd be younger," he said. "Why are you here?"

Jeri stiffened. "I told you. This is my land and—"

"Half yours."

"All right. Half mine." She stared at Wade openly, and he saw her gold-brown eyes darken as she watched him. She had a ripe mouth, the lower lip soft and moist and full.

"I know you were my dad's partner," Jeri said. "When he left me his half of the land and house, I didn't realize you lived here. I guess I should have checked."

"Guess you should have." Wade felt a twinge of regret at his abruptness as he noticed the faint purple hollows under her eyes. Weakly, she raked her slim fingers through her hair. Poor thing looked pretty well tuckered out, Wade decided, but that wasn't his problem. As a matter of fact, he had quite enough problems without a spoiled city girl barging in to check out her inheritance. It was bad enough that O'Brian had willed his half of the partnership to her—land, house, mining claim, the whole enchilada. It had never occurred to Wade that she would actually show up to claim it.

Great, he thought with disgust. Just great.

"Now what?" Jeri was bone tired. "I was planning to stay here."

Wade gave an annoyed shrug. "Change your plans. Town's back down that road."

"Well, sport, that presents another little problem. You see, my car is about a mile down that little dirt path you call a road and it's deader than a doornail.

Cursing under his breath, Wade glared mercilessly at the bedraggled nymph who was turning an already frustrating day into total disaster. "What's the matter with it?" he asked through tightly clamped teeth.

Weary brown eyes returned his fierce stare with unwavering intensity. "I don't have the vaguest idea. What's more, mister, at this particular moment, I don't even care. I've been traveling for over nine hours straight. All I want is a tall glass of water and a place to lie down." Jeri turned around to pick up a large, well-worn leather suitcase and trudged doggedly toward the front door of the cabin.

"Where do you think you're going?"

"I'm going into my half of the house and get a drink of water from my half of the faucet. Then I'm going to sleep," she called as she disappeared through the doorway.

Wade stared after her in astonishment. The little vixen was moving right in—was actually *inside* his house. She just picked up her suitcase and walked through the front door like she owned it.

No way.

Jerome O'Brian, you son of an Irish devil, he fumed silently. *Was this your idea of a joke?*

Wade continued his mental tirade, reaching the doorway of the cabin in two long strides and following the sound of clunking cupboard doors into the kitchen.

Jeri was standing on bare tiptoes opening the overhead cabinets one by one in an apparent search for a glass. Wade watched as she located the proper vessel, filled it and drained it avidly, moaning as the cool liquid washed down her obviously parched throat. Then she turned on the faucet, scooping handfuls of water to splash across her face, smoothing it over her cheeks and throat as though it were fifty-dollar-an-ounce moisturizing lotion. Eyes closed, lips half smiling, she threw her head back and seemed to purr with pleasure.

Wade's mesmerized eyes followed a fat drop of water as it slid from the hollow of her throat over her breastbone to disappear in the valley between her breasts.

Suddenly Jeri's eyes flashed open and met his look of frank appraisal with one of surprise. With a snort of angry embarrassment, Wade whirled and strode back into the living room, stopping in front of the large window by the front door. He stood there looking out, big arms wound tightly across his chest.

It had been nearly six months since his partner's death. In eight years, O'Brian hadn't had a single word from his daughter. Now, without a lick of warning, this dark-haired sprite appears on Wade's doorstep to stake her claim. Next, she would want to know how Jerome O'Brian had died.

And why Wade had let it happen.

He kicked at a dry leaf on the floor and wondered how Jerome O'Brian, with a face like weathered bedrock, could have sired a sweet-looking woman like that. Maybe she was an impostor.

Wade heard Jeri enter the living room and nervously clear her throat. At the sound, his body stiffened, rippling the muscles across his shoulders until they strained against his shirt.

"I'm sorry." She sounded tired. "We seem to have gotten off on the wrong foot."

Wade continued to stare silently out the window.

"I'm normally not so... cranky. It's just that I've had a really lousy day and..." Her voice trailed off as she stared at his rigid back. With a deep breath, she tried again. "I'd like for us to be friends. When I finally saw my dad last winter, he told me you were the best partner a man could have... and the best friend. I know he would have wanted us to get along...."

Wade turned his head slightly, eyes narrowed. She seemed to shrink under his ominous expression. "You don't know one blasted thing about what your daddy wanted." He watched with satisfaction as the color drained from her face.

"What do you mean?"

Swearing under his breath, Wade faced her. "Not one word from you in eight years, not even a postcard. Now he's gone and you show up all full of daughterly devotion. If you want to soothe your conscience by spouting that garbage for other folks, fine, but I don't buy it."

With two strides and a savage yank, Wade threw the cabin door open then marched angrily toward his blue pickup. The dog jumped into the cab, and Wade followed, slamming the truck door. When he looked toward the cabin, he saw Jeri standing in the doorway, a stunned expression on her face. She looked like a doe staring down the muzzle of a loaded Winchester, and her vulnerability increased Wade's irritation.

"I'm going to fix your car, lady." He glowered through the open window. "When I get back, I expect you to get in it and go."

Roughly shoving the truck into gear, he yanked the wheel and stomped the accelerator. A cloud of dust and leaves fluttered in his wake as the truck disappeared down the road.

Deepening frustration replaced Jeri's dazed numbness. She turned back into the cabin and pushed the coarse plank door closed behind her.

"Well," she muttered to herself. "That went nicely."

It was her own fault, she knew. All of her life, Jeri had proceeded toward her goals logically, carefully and with dogged determination. Even when her father had suddenly reappeared last winter and begged her to join him here in the valley, Jeri had been wary of giving up her secure, though uninspiring, bookkeeping position. Jerome had always been a dreamer; Jeri had always been a realist, but before he'd left again, she'd found herself promising to think about it.

And while she had been thinking, Jerome O'Brian had died.

The letter from Jerome's lawyer had been very nice, very sympathetic, very businesslike. She had lost a father and gained a partner. Wade Evans.

So without a backward glance or a thought to the future, Jeri had packed up her life and come to Gold Creek in a gesture that was too little, too late.

Jeri gave her beleaguered suitcase an angry kick. It lurched backward, and she winced in pain, grabbing at her bruised bare foot. "Nice going." She limped across the living room. "Break your foot. That'll solve all your problems." She dropped into one of two oversize recliners and fought the overwhelming urge to indulge in a loud, satisfying primal scream.

Instead, she continued to mutter aloud. "You salty old leprechaun. You forgot to mention a few things, didn't you?"

O'Brian had told her about his partner, all right. He'd said Evans had property all over the valley, but had forgotten to mention that he actually lived at Gold Creek. Jeri had pictured Evans as an older man, nearer her father's age. She certainly hadn't figured him to be in his early thirties with a set of pecs that could shame a bodybuilder.

Jeri yawned and stretched. Yessirree, she thought sleepily. Nice body. Rotten disposition but definitely a nice body.

A horrendous crash reverberated through the cabin. Half leaping out of the chair in groggy panic, Jeri grasped at the padded leather armrest. The front door was slightly ajar, still vibrating from the forceful slam. Blinking to clear her sleep-dazed eyes, Jeri gradually became aware of a gruff male voice drifting from the kitchen.

"Arnie? Ben there? Yeah...."

Mr. Wonderful was back, thought Jeri irritably. Still, she strained to hear every word, eavesdropping shamelessly on his telephone conversation.

"Ben? Need a tow. No, tomorrow's too late...got a car blocking my road...what?...hell, I didn't look. It's the only car out there, Ben." Wade's voice was tinged with annoyance. "About three miles up. Okay...thanks."

Jeri heard the receiver replaced with a distinctive thunk and quickly leaned back in the chair, assuming an expression of feigned indifference. She waited quietly for Wade to come into the living room and offer a report on the status of her vehicle. After several silent minutes had passed, Jeri heard the sound of the refrigerator door followed by the coarse grate of a wooden chair sliding across the floor.

Obviously, Mr. Evans was not particularly anxious to discuss anything. As she saw it, she had two choices. She could trot into the kitchen indignantly and say, "Well?" or she could close her eyes and try to get a few more minutes' rest before the next round of fireworks. Choosing the latter course of action, Jeri curled back into the chair with a comfortable sigh.

A pleasant, drowsy warmth was spreading over her when she felt a peculiar tingling sensation and opened her eyes. Wade Evans was standing over her. His eyes were veiled, unreadable, and there was a tight clamp to his angular jaw. Over six feet tall, his powerful shoulders made him appear even larger, and Jeri shivered under his unwavering stare. The damp brown bottle he thrust toward her was nearly concealed by his massive hand.

"Beer?" His voice was as expressionless as his face.

"No, thank you. I don't care for beer."

He shrugged nonchalantly, put her bottle on the end table then lowered himself into the remaining recliner, filling it to capacity. He sat silently, alternately swigging from his bottle and staring darkly across at Jeri.

"My car..." She was getting nervous. "Do you know what's wrong with it?"

Wade took another long swallow. "Transmission, probably."

Jeri nodded as though she understood completely. "Will it take long to fix?"

"Depends."

"Depends on what?"

"On what's wrong with it," he said, obviously irritated. "Ben will let me know tomorrow. Then I'll let *you* know."

"Yes...of course." Jeri had a deepening sense of impending doom. "Do you have any idea how much it might cost?"

Wade fixed her with an exasperated look. "Depends."

"Right," Jeri said crisply, and folded her arms tightly across her chest. Lord deliver her from tight-lipped mountain men.

Dwarfed by the chair, she curled up in a ball, grasping her knees tightly under her chin like a small, dark-haired kitten. As she glanced curiously around the room, Jeri saw that all of the walls were paneled with light-colored knotty pine, shining slightly from a thin coat of clear protective lacquer. Huge, rough-hewed timber beams supported a wood plank ceiling, and the massive fireplace was constructed of large, jagged, many-hued rocks.

"My father built this cabin, didn't he?"

"We were partners. We built it together." The bottle rolled in his hand. "Just like we owned the land together."

The emphasis wasn't lost on Jeri. "I'm aware of that." She managed a smile. "I guess you're a bit disappointed in his replacement."

"Guess I am."

Well, she'd asked for that.

"You can't sell out, you know." Wade's mouth was tight. "It's in the contract. The land can't be divided, and it can't be sold without the consent of both partners."

Jeri blinked. "Why would I want to sell?"

He gave a humorless smile before taking another swig of beer. "The usual reasons. Money."

"I see." Jeri studied her fingernails. "You can relax, Mr. Evans. I don't want to sell." She looked up and eyed him squarely. "In fact, I'd like to buy you out."

Wade's fingers whitened around the bottle. "Forget it."

"I'm prepared to offer—"

"I said forget it." He stood abruptly, paced across the room, then turned to fix Jeri with a hard stare. "Lady, I don't know why you've showed up, but I'll tell you right now, you've got no business here. Just because your name is on some piece of paper, don't think you can come waltzing in here, tearing up everything your daddy worked for."

"What? I just told you—"

"Why'd you come here anyway? Land? You can't sell it. Gold?" His laugh was unpleasant. "You couldn't pull enough gold out of that creek by yourself to plate a pinhead. So what are you doing here?"

She looked up, her eyes filled with confusion and unhappiness. When she spoke, her voice was so soft he had to strain to hear. "I honestly don't know," she whispered. "I guess I was looking for something."

Wade watched her in sullen silence.

"Daddy and I didn't know each other too well," Jeri said. "It seems he was always coming and going, but when I was fourteen, he left and didn't come back anymore. When he showed up last winter, you could've knocked me over." She laughed. "He hadn't changed a bit. He always loved my paintings and said he'd found the perfect place for me to pursue my art career."

Wade raised an eyebrow. "Gold Creek?"

"Yes." She smiled sadly. "'"Tis truly God's country, Jeri lass,' he said. 'All that splendor just waiting for you to capture on canvas. Think of it, girl!' He made it sound like a paradise." Her glance traveled to the window as she whispered, "And it is."

"He asked you to come here?"

Jeri nodded. "Yes. That's why I just assumed that he lived here alone."

"But you didn't come."

"I said I'd think about it." She lifted her hand in a gesture that requested understanding. "He'd always been so...so unpredictable, you see. I was wary of just dropping everything. I mean, what if he left me again?"

Wade rubbed his forehead. This was getting complex. "So just what is it you're looking for?"

"Answers, I guess." She curled her fingers into her palms. "He was always leaving me, and I want to know why. Suddenly, he comes to get me and I want to know why." Her fists tightened. "Now he's dead, *and I want to know why*."

Wade winced and turned away. Jeri saw a glint of something in his eyes. It looked like fear.

"Some things are best left alone," he said.

"What does that mean?"

He shrugged stiffly. "Digging up the past never did anyone any good." His voice held a warning. "You'd do well to remember that, lady."

"Thank you for the advice." She straightened. "Now, where's the bedroom?"

Wade's eyes narrowed. "Why?"

"You may not have noticed, but I *am* a bit tired."

A small flicker of panic etched Wade's expression. "Don't get comfortable. You're not staying."

Without a word, Jeri rose from the chair, shoulders squared and chin high. She threw Wade a challenging look, then walked over and picked up her suitcase, carrying it into the narrow hallway. She located the bathroom and two bedrooms. The first bedroom was cluttered and untidy. A pair of rumpled socks lay strewed on the floor, and Jeri assumed this was Wade's room.

The other bedroom was neat and clean, almost sterile. A picture of a very young, very familiar girl stared back at her from the oak dresser. Jeri set her suitcase on the bed and picked up the photograph, feeling the moist heat collect in her eyes.

Jeri had been in eighth grade, braces on her teeth and all, when the picture was taken. It had been the year before her father left that last and final time. Jeri hadn't even known he'd brought this picture with him, but here it was, after all these years. She smiled. A small tear skimmed her cheek.

"You've changed a lot since then," Wade said from the doorway. He leaned casually against the frame, thumbs hooked in his jeans pockets. He saw her tears and fought the urge to scoop her protectively into his arms.

Wiping at her wet cheek, Jeri managed a smile. "I'm glad you didn't get rid of it with the rest of his things. It means a lot to me to know he kept it all this time."

"I didn't throw anything of Jerome's away. Everything's just the way he left it. Except it's cleaner."

Jeri looked up in surprise and was further astonished to see a flash of quick pain darken Wade's face. He really misses him, thought Jeri. Wade had honestly cared about Jerome O'Brian.

Wade fidgeted. "Now that you're here, I guess he'd want you to have it." Thinking about Jerome made him feel emotions, and emotions made Wade uncomfortable. "There's some stuff in the closet. Set out what you want and you can bring it to the motel."

Confused, Jeri looked up. "Motel?"

"Ben should have the road clear in another hour. Then I'll take you on into town," Wade said with exaggerated patience. "Now go on and get it ready to go."

Jeri walked to the closet and opened it. Lovingly she fingered the few worn shirts hanging there. Some work boots lay abandoned on the floor, a pair of tennis shoes with a huge hole in the left toe, a cardboard storage box...the meager acquisitions of a lifetime.

Jeri bent to pick up a small glass bottle from the corner of the closet floor. "Daddy pulled one of these out of his pocket, and it had a tiny bit of dust in it. He swelled up like a peacock over that little bit of gold."

Wade watched her bite her lip, then stare wistfully at the small bottle in her hand before slipping it into her pocket. He followed her glance to the cardboard box on the closet floor. It was about two feet square, the edges flattened and tucked over the top.

"What's in the box?" she asked.

"Don't know. I never looked."

Jeri glanced at Wade, her eyes mirroring a silent question.

"Sure," Wade answered. "Go ahead."

The box appeared surprisingly lightweight. Jeri lifted it easily, setting it in the middle of the bedroom floor. She tugged at one flap until it came loose, then opened the box and peered inside.

Wade saw her expression change from bewilderment to shock. She reached in and pulled out what appeared to be a large stack of letters, neatly bound with a rubber band. She pulled out three more stacks of similar size, then sat on the floor and arranged the piles in front of her. He saw the color drain from Jeri's face as she pulled one letter out of the nearest stack, delicately tracing the outline of the sprawling, handwritten address on the envelope.

"It's to me," she whispered. "They're all to me."

Wade's breath slid out in a long, slow whistle. "Well dang his hide. That fool Irishman never *did* mail them."

Wade walked to the middle of the room, then squatted on his haunches as he surveyed the neat mounds. There were at least a dozen letters in each one. He picked up one bundle and saw that each envelope was sealed, addressed to Jeri in San Francisco and bore no return address. Wade had watched Jerome meticulously labor over these letters through the years. No wonder he'd never gotten an answer.

Jeri's eyes were cavernous, widened against the stark white of her skin. She stared incomprehensibly at the small white envelope in her hand.

"Didn't you ever hear from him?" Wade's voice was gentle.

She shook her head slowly. A small shudder vibrated her slumped shoulders, and she wiped at her face with the back of a trembling hand. "Why didn't he mail these? It would have meant so much to know that he was thinking about me." Jeri looked up at Wade, eyes rounded in confusion, glistening with unshed tears. "I wish...I wish I'd come with him when he asked me to." Her voice was husky, almost imploring Wade to understand something that even she couldn't quite comprehend. Seemingly without conscious thought, she extended her palm in a gesture of helplessness.

Wanting to comfort her, Wade touched her shoulder, squeezing it lightly before moving to massage the corded muscles of her neck. She smelled good, he thought. Sweet, like a springtime meadow.

She looked up, surprise and gratitude reflected in her soft expression. Eyes like a fawn, Wade decided. A trusting fawn smiling at the wolf that's sizing her up for lunch.

His hand dropped abruptly. These thoughts were way out of line. Wade firmly reminded himself that this woman was his partner's daughter.

"Were you with him?" Jeri asked.

"When?"

"When...it happened."

"Oh." Wade didn't want to talk about this, and his answer was gruff. "Yes."

Jeri seemed deep in thought for several moments. Then she hesitated, as though trying to form her words.

Anticipating her question, Wade answered it succinctly before she asked. "It was fast. He didn't feel any pain."

Jeri closed her eyes. "Thank you." She took several deep breaths, as though to compose herself, then leveled her unwavering stare on Wade. "Why didn't you call me?"

Startled, Wade dropped the envelope he held. "What?"

"When Daddy...died, why didn't you call me? Why did you let me find out a month later from an impersonal letter by some faceless attorney?" She gave him an impaling gaze, but her eyes misted. "I didn't even know about the funeral."

Guilt tightened Wade's chest. He could lie, try to convince Jeri that he didn't know where she was or how to reach her, but Wade owed her the truth. Well, part of it, anyway. He matched her stare. "Because I didn't think you'd care."

Jeri's hand went to her throat, as though to catch the tiny gasp.

"I can see I was wrong. I'm sorry." He pushed the cardboard carton toward her. "Why don't you finish going through the box," he urged, hoping to break the somber mood. "It might make you feel better."

With a somewhat listless nod, she reached into the carton and pulled out a manila envelope. It was filled with old pictures of days when the O'Brians had been a family. Wade watched the crisp images of happier times cause Jeri to choke up, and he found a lump in his own throat. The weakness irritated him immensely.

The box also contained several vials of gold in varying sizes, from small nuggets and flakes to flour-fine dust. Jeri held one of the bottles, her eyes widened in awe. "What would these be worth?"

Wade's mouth twisted in a wry, knowing smile. "Depends on how much it weighs." There's the heart of it, he decided. Gold. Green or yellow, money's the name of a woman's game. This one was probably no different. Wade saw her eyes light at the color of gold. It would be half hers now, what there was of it. He wondered if half would be enough for her.

"It's so beautiful," Jeri whispered, reverently placing the small jars back into the box. She picked up a stack of letters.

Thoughts of her greedy motives were hastily pushed aside, and Wade's throat seemed to constrict as he watched. He was fascinated by her, by the ethereal glow in her eyes as she touched Jerome's letters. His gaze was drawn to the flash of white teeth nervously scraping across her lower lip. She nibbled absently, obviously lost in thought.

"I'm truly sorry to inconvenience you, Mr. Evans," she said finally, "but I'm not going into town. I'm staying here, in my father's room."

Wade froze. "Lady, that just isn't a very smart idea."

"Smart or not, Mr. Evans, I'm staying." She turned to face him fully. "I understand that you have several properties in the valley. All I have is half of this one, and I'm staying."

They stared at each other, eyes testing, probing, searching for weakness . . . or strength.

Finally Wade took a long, slow breath. "One of us is liable to be real sorry about that decision."

"Is that a threat, Mr. Evans?" Jeri was instantly alert.

"No, ma'am. It's a warning."

Chapter Two

Wade straightened, turned abruptly and walked briskly out of the bedroom. As Jeri watched him, an ominous prickling sensation played across the back of her neck. For a few moments the enigmatic Wade Evans had seemed almost human, then his eyes had hardened.

There was a depth to this man. Jeri knew it instinctively. She'd had a glimpse of his gentler side, seen compassion mirrored in his eyes as he'd tried to comfort her. There was definitely a soft core of human feeling buried beneath that hard shell of machismo.

With an exasperated sigh, Jeri picked up one of the precious bundles and settled on the bed to read. She had just opened the first envelope when a movement in the hallway caught her eye.

"Well, hello there," she said, smiling.

Murphy sat politely in the doorway, huge brown eyes watching her, as though patiently awaiting an invitation. Jeri's smile broadened as Murphy cocked his head questioningly.

"Yes, of course, you may." Jeri laughed as the dog immediately padded in, leaping on the bed to settle comfortably beside her. Circling once to secure just the right position, Murphy finally flopped himself down, placing his muzzle on neatly crossed forepaws with a contented sigh. He looked up at Jeri with devoted adoration.

"You're a sly one, you are." Jeri stroked his sleek head. "Too bad your master's not as friendly."

Tucking her legs under her, Jeri settled back and unfolded the first letter. She read for hours, until dusk grayed the room and blurred the words. It was nearly eight, but she wasn't finished. She reached over to turn on the nightstand lamp, clicking it several times when it refused to light.

"Must need a new bulb," she mumbled aloud. Murphy opened one sleepy eye, but the weight of the lid seemed too much for him, and it slammed shut once more.

"I know how you feel." Jeri's eyes were burning fiercely. She decided to rest them for a few minutes before facing her scowling host to ask for another light bulb. Just a few minutes. Then she would feel much better.

It was nearly midnight when Wade came to the door holding a glowing oil lamp. He surveyed the scene. Letters were scattered around and over the large double bed, and in the middle of the clutter lay Jeri, sound asleep, one slim arm tossed possessively across the snoring animal.

She must own half the dog, too, thought Wade dryly.

He set the lamp on the dresser and searched the closet shelf for a spare blanket. Finding it, he spread it gently over her. Murphy yawned and looked up.

"Lucky devil," Wade muttered.

Stretching lazily, Murphy took a deep breath and closed his eyes. Wade could swear that darn dog was smiling.

Morning broke harshly, bright rays penetrating Jeri's sleep-heavy eyelids, insisting she greet the new day. After stumbling around the unfamiliar surroundings, she found the bathroom and splashed her face thoroughly with cold, invigorating water. She straightened the bedroom, carefully bundling her precious letters and storing them back in the cardboard carton.

Jeri picked up the blanket, smiling softly as she folded it and laid it neatly at the foot of the bed. Unless that dog was unusually clever, she had one more bit of proof that Wade Evans had a few kind bones in that brawny body.

The cabin was strangely quiet. Jeri walked through the empty living room to the kitchen. Half a pot of still-warm coffee was on the stove, and the aroma of bacon lingered invitingly in the air.

Jeri was starving.

An hour later, Jeri finished washing dishes and clearing away remnants of her three-course breakfast. She felt much better, but her conscience tugged at her. She had helped herself to his food without even the courtesy of asking, and Jeri was not one to expect such favors. Such expectations had been her mother's specialty, and Jeri still abhorred anything remotely resembling charity.

Slipping into a pair of tan shorts and a long-tailed, oversize T-shirt, Jeri tucked some money in her pocket and headed out the door. It was a beautiful day, and she thoroughly enjoyed the exercise. Within an hour, Jeri arrived at the Klamath Valley Store, a small mom-and-pop establishment run by Martha and Jed Turkle. The Turkles were friendly folks, and Jeri liked them both instantly. Martha reminded her of an apple-pie-baking grandma. Jed was a lanky man, bald on top with a tremendous bushy gray beard covering the top part of his chest.

Martha chatted amiably with Jeri, bubbling with excitement when she discovered her to be the daughter of their favorite Irishman. "Jerome O'Brian's girl!" gushed Martha. "How that man bragged on you. Are you still painting?"

Surprised, Jeri nodded. Jerome had actually spoken of her to his friends . . . bragged about her?

"He was always talking about how talented you are. Where you staying, child?"

Jeri smothered a smile. "Gold Creek."

"Well, now, of course, you are. Right silly of me to ask," Martha bubbled. Jed grunted once, then continued to bag Jeri's groceries in solemn silence.

The chance for precious information was too much to pass up. "Did you know my father well?" Jeri asked.

"As well as anyone," Martha replied. "He stayed to himself, mostly. Took off a lot, as I recall. Sometimes he'd disappear for weeks at a time, then suddenly show up all chipperlike. Everyone liked him, though. He was real helpful to those that needed him. That'll be eight-fifty."

Jeri dug into her pocket, thanked Martha and hoisted two grocery bags. "Do you know where Ben's garage is?" Jeri asked. If it was close by, maybe her car would be ready.

Martha pursed her lips, frowning. "Garage? No, I don't think so."

"Gas station," Jed said. "Ben Hawkins's gas station down at Humbug Creek."

"Humbug Creek? How far's that?"

"Not far. Maybe fifteen, twenty miles."

Jeri's heart sank. So much for that idea.

Martha was instantly concerned. "What's wrong? You got trouble with your car?"

Jeri nodded. "It died on me yesterday. Wade had it towed to Ben's. I was hoping it was ready so I didn't have to carry these groceries back up that blasted road."

"Carry? Why, you'll do no such thing. Jed'll be glad to take you, won't you, Jed?" Martha smiled sweetly up at the tall man. Jed grunted twice.

"Oh, no . . . please, that's not necessary. I wasn't fishing for a ride . . . really." Jeri could feel the crimson flush start up her cheeks. In the city, her comment about carrying gro-

ceries would have brought only bland stares or empathetic
nods.

"No trouble," stated Jed. "Come on."

He scooped the groceries out of Jeri's arms, and she
meekly followed him to his truck, sheepishly waving goodbye to a beaming Martha.

In twenty minutes she was standing in front of the cabin
thanking Jed Turkle for the lift. She noted that Wade's truck
was still gone and went in to kick off her hated shoes and put
the groceries away. Setting the bags on the kitchen counter,
she glanced out the window and saw a small, furry creature
bustling around the base of a Douglas fir about thirty feet
from the house. Then another one appeared and scam-
pered quickly up the tree.

Delighted, Jeri dashed to get her sketchpad and quietly
found a spot outside where she could watch without disturbing them. Skillfully wielding fat sticks of charcoal, she
quick-sketched the squirrels in various poses. In a half hour
she had covered several sheets, but was still disappointed
when the little animals suddenly sat up, sniffed the air and
scurried up the trunk to disappear in the boughs of the tree.

Jeri heard Wade's truck engine a few moments before it
pulled into the clearing. She stood up, dusted her rear and
walked toward the cabin. As soon as Wade opened the truck
door, the big dog jumped out and ran toward Jeri, leaping
happily up to place his huge paws on her shoulders.

"Murphy, dammit! Behave yourself," Wade growled,
and Murphy reluctantly sat at her feet.

"Murphy? So that's your name. It suits you."

Wade was standing beside her. "What's that?" He
pointed to her sketchpad.

"Oh. Squirrel sketches. I made a few quick drawings."
She handed the pad to Wade, and he slowly flipped the
pages, carefully studying each pose.

"Not bad," he said, almost grudgingly, as he handed the
sketchpad back.

Tilting her head to acknowledge the reluctant compliment, Jeri managed a shy smile before heading back to the kitchen.

As she resumed unloading her groceries she wondered why in the world Wade's terse commentary made her feel warm all over. Certainly he was no major art critic, so why did Wade's opinion mean anything at all to her? Why was it important that he approve of her work—and of her?

Jeri was mentally mulling these meaty issues when she felt, rather than heard, Wade's presence in the kitchen. Pulling her head out of the open refrigerator, a quick look over her shoulder confirmed her hunch. He didn't look particularly happy, but it seemed to Jeri that he hadn't been particularly happy since she arrived.

No way was a sourpuss sourdough going to disturb her happy mood. Jeri was determined to be friendly no matter what. She made her voice decisively cheerful. "Have a nice morning?"

Wade scrutinized her like a fire fighter watching an arsonist, narrowed eyes glancing from the grocery bags to her activity at the refrigerator.

"What are you doing?" he demanded, ignoring her question completely.

"As you can see, Mr. Evans," she said through cheerfully clamped teeth, "I'm putting away groceries."

"Wade—just Wade. Why?"

Jeri took a deep breath. Calm. Cheerful. Happy.

"Because, Wade, some things will spoil if you leave them on the counter. Eggs, bacon, hamburger...that kind of thing. If you put them in the refrigerator, they last longer." Jeri smiled sweetly. "Can you understand that?"

Wade's expression darkened ominously, and Jeri instantly regretted her sarcasm. This man could break her like a dry stick if he wanted, and she was behaving like a first-class, smart-mouth brat. Unable to meet his angry stare, Jeri lowered her eyes, clearing her throat nervously.

She spoke softly. "That wasn't very nice of me. I apologize."

Wade's eyebrows arched in surprise. A woman who admits she was wrong? Interesting.

"I was hungry this morning and took some of your food. I should have asked..." Jeri looked up and smiled tentatively, "but I was really starving."

"So you ate breakfast. So what?"

"Of course, I replaced it, and I got my own groceries."

"You did what?"

"I...replaced it."

"No, after that." He flicked his hand impatiently.

"What?" Jeri looked bewildered. "I got my own groceries?"

"That's the part. I thought sure I heard you wrong." Wade walked to the kitchen table, turned a solid wooden chair around with a deft flick of his wrist and straddled it backward, resting his arms comfortably on top of the backrest. Then he simply watched her. Intensely. For a long, long time.

Attempting to ignore his stare, Jeri proceeded to unconsciously shred a paper towel into a thick rain of puckered confetti. Finally Wade's gaze dropped to the pile of paper bits on the linoleum. Jeri followed his gaze, flushing to her scalp as she hastily brushed the scraps into her hand and disposed of them. Turning her back on him, she busied herself by tucking the remaining groceries quickly out of sight.

"Just how long are you planning to stay?" Wade asked when she had finished.

"For a while."

The heavy silence was palpable.

"How long a while?"

Jeri shrugged. "The cabin is half mine." She gave him a honeyed smile. "You'll hardly notice I'm here."

Wade seemed to cogitate that thought for several seconds before he spoke again, his voice deceptively even.

"Lady, I guarantee I'll notice, but I'm going to be fair about this situation."

His massive frame loomed above the chair as he stood and walked slowly toward the refrigerator to get a beer. When he had taken a couple of deliberate swallows, he returned to the chair, swinging his leg over it to resume his former position.

"Stopped by Ben's on my way back from Yreka. Seems your car's in pretty bad shape. It'll be out of commission for at least a week."

Alarmed, Jeri stiffened quickly at the unsettling news, opening her mouth to ask a question. Holding up a callused palm, Wade made it clear he was not finished talking. "I figure you could use a little vacation, so I'm going to let you stay here while Ben fixes your car."

Wade ignored Jeri's sullen expression and the dangerous glint in her dark eyes. In fact, he broke into a smile. The effect was startling. Lines crinkling at the edge of his eyes seemed to point directly at the multicolored glow flickering from bright, iridescent irises. Two deep grooves etched his face from cheekbone to jaw, and white teeth flashed invitingly from behind a perfectly molded mouth.

"You're a bright woman. By then, you'll have figured out that you don't belong here." His grin widened. "Then I'll buy your share, and you can go on home. Fair enough?"

Jeri didn't answer immediately. Instead, she walked slowly to the refrigerator and took her time in removing a can of soda. When she turned around, Wade's smile began to fade. Mimicking Wade's earlier behavior, Jeri also took two deliberate swallows, then walked to the table and pulled out a chair. When comfortably seated, she smiled across at him.

"Tell me about my car, Wade."

Furrowing his tanned forehead, Wade seemed to concentrate intently on the wet beer bottle, using his thumb to roll it slowly along the palm of his hand. He was aware that by smoothly changing the subject she avoided further discussion on the length of her stay. He also assumed, correctly, that she was not nearly ready to give up her claim. Stubborn, just like her daddy.

"Wade? My car?"

"What? Oh. What about it?"

"Well, for starters, what's wrong with it?"

"Transmission's shot." His voice was gruffer than he intended, and he softened his tone. "Ben'll drop the trans and send it up to Medford. A place there rebuilds them."

Jeri scratched at a blemish in the oak tabletop. "Did he mention how much this might cost?"

"Six-fifty. Seven, tops."

Eyes rounding in shock, her pupils seem to retract into tiny black pinholes in huge, penny-colored irises. Her voice was a husky whisper. "Seven hundred dollars? Are you joking?"

Wade's brows ruffled. "Don't you have any money?"

"Of course, I do." Her heart sank at the news. She did have some savings, but it wasn't going to last long at this rate. Besides, she had plans for that money. It was the key to her future, her new life. "I just didn't expect a little repair job to be so much."

"It isn't such a little job, lady. Ben's giving you a good deal because you're O'Brian's kid. That even includes the towing."

"Jeri!" Her voice was sharp and loud enough to startle Wade. "My name is Jeri." She was instantly embarrassed by her outburst as well as the amused glint in Wade's eye.

"Lady is a dog's name," she muttered under her breath.

To her surprise, the comment brought a deep rumble of laughter from across the table.

"Well . . . Jeri. You're no dog, and that's a fact."

Wade's good-natured grin was contagious, and Jeri joined in with a self-conscious snort that tickled her even more. Soon they were both grinning and giggling at the preposterous situation, and the tense moment was effectively diffused.

Finally Wade stood, returning the chair to the table with an effortless flick and tossing the empty bottle into the trash container.

"Guess I've sat enough." He seemed reluctant to leave. "I've got chores that won't do themselves."

"Oh, sure." Jeri stood quickly. "I wanted to finish my letters this morning. It got too dark last night to—oh, darn!"

Stopping midway in his stride, Wade turned to look at Jeri curiously.

"I forgot to buy a light bulb at the store. The one in my room is burned out."

"Nothing's wrong with the bulb."

"Well, it won't light," Jeri pointed out.

"Still nothing wrong with it. No electricity. Generator's down."

Jeri blinked at Wade in disbelief. "That doesn't make any sense. The refrigerator's working, everything's cold in there."

"Gas."

"I beg your pardon?"

"Gas," he repeated. "Liquid propane. Tank's out back."

"Oh."

Wade continued to speak as he walked toward the front door. Jeri followed, listening, taking two quick steps to every one of his long strides.

"... Having a part made. It'll be ready in a couple of days," he said. "Then I'll take another crack at putting it back together."

"I hope we have plenty of candles."

"Your confidence is appreciated, ma'am."

Stopping abruptly in the open doorway, Wade turned toward her. "By the way, where did you . . . ?"

She was closer than he'd realized. The question died on his lips as he stood staring at her, scrutinizing with an intensity so powerful, so unexpected that he saw her breathing become momentarily disrupted. He noticed the quick rise of her chest with her sharp intake of breath, noted the subtle stiffening of her shoulders, and knew instinctively that she was as affected by his presence as he was by hers.

And with that knowledge, a deep craving ripped at him like a dull-toothed saw, because he knew he wouldn't—couldn't—give in to it.

She was alone, afraid and vulnerable to him. Wade knew she was probably here searching for riches, a literal gold digger. Still, she was O'Brian's daughter. He had a duty to his old friend, an obligation he didn't take lightly. The crusty Irishman loved this girl and would have expected Wade to move heaven and earth to help her, not bed her. If he touched one silky hair on Jeri's head, Wade was certain that Jerome's ghost would swoop down and haunt him to the end of his days.

Jeri's eyes had widened, her pulse racing erratically, affected by the intense power of his unwavering stare. Wade had the look of a man at war with himself, the turmoil of his internal struggle etched in deep creases slashing across his face like trenches on a battlefield. She watched, transfixed, his eyes exposing his inner conflict. Then the veil dropped, masking his feelings with a protective, unreadable curtain.

Just as suddenly as it had begun, the spell was broken, its only legacy the husky tremor of his voice. "Where...did you get those groceries?"

"I...ah...at the store."

"The nearest store is six miles," he said. "How did you get there?"

"I walked."

Wade stared down at her bare feet and wondered if this woman ever wore shoes. "That's a long way."

Jeri detected a hint of approval in his voice. "It wasn't too bad. Jed Turkle brought me back."

Wade was apprehensive. "Talk to Martha?"

Jeri nodded. "She's a nice lady. She knew who I was...she said Daddy actually *bragged* about me, about my painting." Her eyes glowed with pleasure. "I can hardly believe it."

Wade's breath left in a slow, steady sigh. "Well, you can believe that the whole valley'll know you're here by suppertime."

Jeri was surprised by his reaction. "Is something wrong with that?" She relaxed only slightly as Wade shook his head.

"Guess not." He managed a weak smile. "Tongues are going to wag, though. Play hell with my saintly reputation."

Good grief. It hadn't even occurred to Jeri that staying under the same roof with Wade would naturally give rise to all manner of speculation. Especially in a place as close-knit as the valley.

"What about *my* reputation?" she asked with growing alarm.

Wade's smile broke into a devastating, face-splitting, grin. "You don't want to know," he said cheerfully, then headed out the door, his deep, soft chuckle drifting back to assault Jeri's already flaming ears.

Muttering peevishly to herself, she went back to her room—and her letters.

Jerome's letters were more of a diary, a periodic log of his life over the past ten years. Jeri suspected that he never even planned to mail them; that he left them to say all the things he couldn't bring himself to express while he was alive. For the first time, she began to understand much of what made her father tick, what driving force propelled him. Jeri realized that her own sense of betrayal had blinded her, made her bitterly reject what her mother had told her all along.

Jerome O'Brian was a dreamer. He dreamed of the world as it was a hundred years ago. Literally, he was born too late, unable to be assimilated into a fast-paced, materialistic world, and it nearly destroyed him.

A secret guilt had gnawed Jeri for years, a gut-wrenching fear that her father had left because he no longer loved her, because his only child had somehow disappointed him. After reading the letters, Jeri felt a sense of relief.

Perhaps he really *had* loved her, hadn't rejected a daughter, but a life-style. She cried silent tears for the fate that had brought him back to her so briefly, only to sweep him away once more, hopelessly, forever.

Perhaps she would never really know who Jerome O'Brian was or, as his daughter, who she was. But she was driven to search for answers, and Jeri was certain those answers were here—at Gold Creek.

Jeri blew her nose, then went into the bathroom to splash away the visible remnants of her grief. The tepid water cooled her fevered skin but couldn't fill that void lingering deep inside her.

Jeri went to the living room. A pinkish glow bathed the air, mute signal of impending twilight. She saw Wade through the window, powerfully slamming a huge-headed hammer onto a metal cone deeply wedged in the meat of a fat log. He was using a large tree stump, about two feet across, as a base. Again and again, he pounded the wedge until the log split with a groaning crack, its halves falling heavily off the stump into the soft dirt.

He'd been working all afternoon, each rhythmic thud reassuring testimony of his presence. Sleeves rolled to above his elbows, Jeri could see the sweat shine across the sinewy flex of his muscles. All that strength, that power. It made Jeri feel safe and protected.

She had an irresistible urge to thank Wade for those warm, fuzzy feelings and to express her gratitude for the years of friendship he'd given her father. The letters detailed the strength of that friendship. O'Brian's respect for and devotion to Wade were evident on every page.

Intuitively, Jeri knew Wade wouldn't take kindly to a highly-charged, emotional scene dripping with sentimentality. But that didn't mean she couldn't communicate her appreciation in other ways.

Like stifling her sarcasm, for instance.

And fixing dinner. Jeri's stomach was beginning to rumble ominously, and she realized she hadn't eaten since breakfast. More than likely, Wade hadn't, either.

After rooting around the kitchen, she decided that the speediest course of action would be to whip up a batch of spaghetti and meatballs. Sauce in a jar, a quick salad, a meal in minutes.

In about half an hour, the deed was done. She laid out the plates and silverware, just completing the chore when the front door opened. Nice timing, she mused.

Wade appeared in the kitchen doorway, scowling slightly and sniffing the air like a giant grizzly on the scent of smoked salmon.

She bit back a smile. "I hope you like spaghetti."

With an indecipherable grunt, he turned away and disappeared into the living room. Jeri watched in stunned silence, not realizing where he had gone until she heard water running in the bathroom. He returned in a few minutes in a clean shirt, hair still damp from the quick rinse, and sat at the table, eyeing Jeri skeptically.

"This from your half or mine?"

"Both. Your spaghetti, my salad."

Wade responded with a satisfied nod. Once the food hit the table, however, Wade attacked it voraciously, his communication limited to hand signals. By the time Jeri finished eating, Wade had polished off two more helpings and washed it down with a quart of milk. She could only watch in amused amazement.

As soon as every trace of edible substance had disappeared from the table, Wade filled the sink with hot, foamy water and began to wash the dishes.

"I'm impressed," Jeri said, searching for a towel.

"Middle drawer," Wade offered helpfully. "Around here, one cooks, the other cleans up. That's the rule."

That sounded reasonable, and Jeri nodded in solemn approval. "Could my father cook?"

Wade grimaced. "Sort of. If it came out of a can he did all right. Otherwise..." He gave a noncommittal shrug.

Jeri laughed softly at the mental image of a domesticated Jerome O'Brian slaving over a hot stove. O'Brian had been the absolute personification of a hard-living mountain man. His weathered face had been covered by a three-inch growth of frizzy white whiskers, above which had loomed a too-large, red-veined nose. Even in the city, Jeri had thought her father resembled a transplant from the 1849 gold fields.

While they finished cleaning the kitchen, dusk settled quickly into night. Wade lit an oil lamp to dispel the graying pall and prepared Murphy's dinner, then called him with a piercing whistle. The big dog appeared instantaneously, bounding into the kitchen and diving into the appetizing bowl of kibble and canned meat.

Wade went into the living room and saw that Jeri had curled up in one of the big armchairs. He sank noiselessly into the other one and enjoyed the peaceful, comfortable silence. It had been a long time since he'd enjoyed a meal as much. Wade silently acknowledged that the company was a big part of his pleasure. She didn't have to cook for him. Heaven knows, he'd been less than courteous to her since she'd arrived, yet she'd repaid his rudeness with generosity.

As Wade watched Jeri, he noticed how young she appeared, how fragile. She was a beautiful young woman and with those huge whiskey-colored eyes, Wade could imagine what a lovely child she must have been. How could Jerome have simply left her? Wade felt a surprising twinge of anger prick him and reminded himself quite firmly that Jeri O'Brian was none of his business. She was his partner's daughter. Period.

Jeri's eyes were nearly closed, her lips parted slightly as her head lolled lazily to one side. She sighed, a deep moaning little whimper that raised goose bumps across the back of Wade's neck. O'Brian's daughter or not, she was still a woman, a fact Wade was excruciatingly aware of.

Well, if he just sat here watching her stretch and moan it was going to be one heck of a long, painful night. He suddenly felt grumpy and irritable. "Finish those letters?"

Jeri's eyes flew open, her head snapping upright at his gruff tone.

"Yes. In fact, you might want to read them. They're kind of a chronicle of his life here."

Wade shifted uncomfortably. "He wrote them for you, not me."

"I think he'd want you to read them. For instance, in one of his first letters he tells about how you two met."

"I know how we met. I was there."

Jeri continued, undaunted by Wade's testy glare. "He wrote that he was mining on one of your claims and you caught him. He also said that anyone else would have taken the gold he'd found and kicked his tail clear back to Yreka, but you told him if he was going to hi-grade, he should learn how to do it right. Then you showed him where to look." Jeri cocked her head. "What does 'hi-grade' mean?"

The soft clicking of toenails on the wooden floor heralded Murphy's arrival. With a jaw-racking yawn, the dog sat down next to Wade's chair, laying his muzzle on Wade's knee and closing his eyes with a contented sigh.

"It means to claim-jump," Wade said unhelpfully, absently scratching the yellow head. "What else did he have to say?"

"Well, his next letter was a few months later, right after you both joined forces to buy this land. He wrote about the two of you building this house." Suddenly Jeri started to laugh.

"What's so funny?"

"That fireplace," she said, vainly attempting to control her mirth. "He wrote that he built it all by himself. Twice."

Wade's lips began to twitch in remembrance. "Dang fool forgot to leave a hole in it. He put the entire chimney up over a solid hearth." He shook his head, grinning. "I had a few problems myself."

"You?" Jeri's eyes sparkled. "I don't believe it."

"Yep. I set the east wall frame up backwards. That's why the closet has a window with a view."

Her jaw sagged. "You're joking."

"You're right." He flashed a devastating grin.

Jeri's eyes widened in appreciation. At least he had a sense of humor, and he'd had her going for a minute. "Those sound like wonderful times," she said wistfully.

Wade sobered. "They were."

"You miss him." It was a flat statement for which no answer was required and none was given.

"He wrote about you in every letter." Jeri's voice was soft, intense. "The saddest of all the letters is the one about when you left."

"Left?" Wade was puzzled.

"You know. When you moved in with that woman . . . he didn't mention her name."

Wade's expression darkened, and he fixed her with a menacing stare. Too late Jeri seemed to realize that this subject was not available for discussion as she tried to extricate herself from the results of her indiscreet remark.

"Of course, he was massively relieved when you came back," she said quickly. "Would you like some coffee? Won't take a minute to fix,"

Wade's mouth had snapped tightly shut, the muscles of his jaw flexing as he clamped his teeth together.

"I'm sorry," Jeri whispered miserably. "I didn't mean to pry...." She stood and would have retreated quickly to her room except that Wade's hand clamped around her wrist, pinning her in place while he rose from the chair to tower above her.

Unceremoniously dumped from his headrest, Murphy cast a cautious eye before judiciously deciding to find a more stable rest area.

Jeri held her breath as the anger in his eyes died, replaced by a resigned sadness.

"It's okay," he said quietly. "It was a long time ago."

But he continued to hold her wrist, as though he just wanted an excuse to touch her.

She was lovely, Wade realized. A natural beauty.

Her hand was resting against his chest, and he could feel the heat of her body. With incredible gentleness, Wade pushed a wayward wisp of hair away from her forehead with his free hand, then traced the contour of her face with his fingertips. Reaching her chin, he cupped it lightly between his thumb and forefinger, tilting her head back slightly.

Bells and whistles seemed to sound in his brain, alarms warning him that if he looked into those dark eyes long enough, his world might just change forever.

He heard Jeri's breath catch in her throat as she slid her hand across his chest, slim fingers lightly brushing the hard muscles as though reveling in the feel of them. He felt his muscles tighten at her touch.

Let her go, Wade's brain told him. *Before it's too late.*

Again, he ignored the ominous warning.

Still cupping her chin, he circled his thumb delicately across her lips, brushing them with a touch more elusive than the fragile flutter of a butterfly's wing. He felt her begin to tremble, to sag against him, heard the soft, sweet moan slip unbidden from deep within her, felt her heart go wild against his chest.

Soft, he thought, and innocent. He could see that innocence in her trusting expression, a look that clearly told him she wanted to be held, to be kissed, but that she was bewildered by her own feelings.

"Sweet thing," he murmured, "you're playing with fire. And I'll burn you, honey. You know I will."

Jeri stared into his eyes as though mesmerized, and he saw his own hunger reflected in her face. If he gave in to that hunger, if he betrayed her trust . . . Wade knew he couldn't live with that decision. She deserved more from him than a betrayal of her innocence.

A deep ache pulsated through his body. He recognized her infatuation with him and realized that she would keep reaching out to him until he could no longer turn away.

His body tightened, like a tautly wound spool of steel wire, every muscle pulsing, vibrating under the force of self-imposed restraint. Stiffly, he dropped his arms and turned from her.

"Wade?" she whispered, reaching toward him. She seemed confused, stunned by his sudden rejection.

His answer was purposely gruff. "Go on to bed."

"I'm not a starry-eyed teenager," she said softly. "I know what's happening between us."

"Maybe." He faced her with an impassive stare. "But I really don't think you want to be another one of my good-time girls."

She looked shocked and stared openmouthed, as though she'd been struck mute. Wade wanted to reach out and caress away the humiliation, but she turned shakily, retreating to the relative safety of her room.

He knew he'd hurt her. He'd been deliberately cruel, but there had been no other way. The fact that it had been for her own good did little to ease his conscience or soothe the surprising sense of loss he'd felt as she walked away.

With a vicious oath, Wade whirled and strode toward the cabin door. Murphy sat there, watching him with large, reproachful eyes.

"You got a problem?" Wade snapped.

The big dog stood, stretching leisurely before he ambled down the hall and scratched at Jeri's door.

"Traitorous mutt."

Wade walked into the cool night and stared up at the star-flecked sky. How could he possibly help O'Brian's daughter if he couldn't keep his darn hands off her?

"Jerome, buddy, you sure picked the wrong man for this job." With an exasperated sigh, he looked up. "I'll do my best, but this would just be a whole lot easier if she looked more like you."

Chapter Three

Y ou're up kind of early this morning." Wade stood in the kitchen doorway, silhouetted by the predawn pall.

Jeri eyed him. In the few days she'd been here, Wade had always been gone before she awakened. "So you *do* sleep here. I was beginning to wonder." She waved lazily toward the stove. "The coffee's ready."

With a grateful grunt, Wade poured himself a cup. They sipped their coffee in silence for a few minutes, then Wade mumbled something unintelligible and headed out the door.

"Hey!" Coffee sloshed on the table as Jeri thunked her cup down and bolted after him. She caught up with him on the porch. "Why are you avoiding me?"

Wade stared down at her. He *was* avoiding her, of course, but it seemed to irritate him to have her confront him with the fact.

From his sullen expression, Jeri realized he wasn't going to answer her, but she hadn't dragged herself up at five-thirty in the morning simply to fix his coffee and watch his dust. She wanted to communicate with the man, for heaven's sake. That wasn't a crime.

"You're gone before the sun rises, pop in long enough to inhale the nutritionally complete and downright delicious dinner that I have managed to put on the table, then disappear again until the wee hours." Jeri took a breath. "What do you *do* all that time?"

Wade's eyes narrowed. "If I wanted my mother, I'd go back to Oregon, and if I wanted a wife, I'd have kept the one I had."

Jeri flushed slightly. "Touché. I guess it's none of my business."

"Smart lady."

"It's just that..." She paused, feeling extremely uncomfortable.

"Spit it out."

"Well, I'd hoped I could go with you today and, ah...I'm kind of stuck here without my car, after all."

Wade was silent for a moment, then asked, "Do you need anything? Supplies, food? I could go into town for you—"

"No, I don't need anything. I really appreciated your getting the art supplies from my car the other day." Jeri cleared her throat. "I thought perhaps we could talk a little."

"About what?" Wade tensed as though he knew perfectly well what Jeri wanted to talk about.

"My father. I know so little about him, about his life the past eight years. As a child, I absolutely adored him." Her voice became animated as she spoke faster. "There's so much you could tell me. Did he ever talk about my mom and me? Did he tell you why he left? Do you know what—"

"Hold on there, woman." Wade plowed frustrated furrows through his hair. "The man loved you, dammit. Isn't that enough?"

"No." Jeri grabbed Wade's arm to keep him from turning away. "No, it's not enough, because I don't understand that kind of love. I'm a part of him," she whispered. "It's important that I know who he was, what he stood for."

"What do you want me to tell you, that your daddy was as lovable as a puppy and just as irresponsible? You already know that, and I doubt it makes you feel any better." At her crestfallen expression, Wade softened. "Look, your pedigree doesn't have anything to do with who you are."

"Yes, it does. How would you feel if you didn't know your own father, if you had no idea what kind of man he really was?"

Wade was quiet a moment, then said, "I'd feel a heck of a lot better if I didn't know he was serving fifteen years for armed robbery."

"Oh, Wade. I'm so sorry."

"That doesn't make me a criminal, does it?"

"No, of course not."

"That's my point." Wade sighed. "Honey, if you'd spend less time worrying about your daddy and more time figuring out who you are and what you stand for, you'd be a whole lot better off. You keep on digging and you might not like what you find."

Jeri's hand dropped from Wade's arm. His words had found their mark.

Somehow, the colors just weren't right. Critically eyeing her palette, Jeri dipped the sable brush lightly into a thick smear of yellow ocher, then mixed it with a liberal dab of olive. Satisfied with the brighter hue, she applied it to her canvas in deft, wrist-flicking twists, highlighting the deeper green shades of her landscape. The painting began to take life as she worked, transferring the tranquil image of mind and eye to her art.

The creek was Jeri's favorite spot, and over the past several days she had captured its essence in charcoal, watercolor and now in oils. Her palette knife scraped the rough canvas skin, removing excess paint to highlight, then applying deep sienna shadows to mold the contour of boulders and rocks haphazardly strewed on the creek bank and faithfully reproduced on her easel.

Pleased with her progress, Jeri set the paint-smeared palette on a rock and walked to the edge of the creek. She slipped off her tennis shoes and sat on a soft, mossy area to dangle her bare feet in the cool water.

She watched a long, multilegged creature painfully pull itself along a dried twig, finally disappearing in a tangle of half-buried oak roots. Jeri sighed. Now she was completely alone.

Strange. Actually, she'd always been basically alone, yet had never felt lonely—until now.

Her thoughts turned to Wade, the man who gave new meaning to the term "silent partner." She wished he'd been silent this morning, but certainly she'd asked for it. He'd seemed to see right through her, realizing before Jeri herself did, that a quest for her father was a thinly veiled search for herself.

Wade. What an enigma. On the outside, he was rough as tree bark and just as abrasive. Yet inside, the true essence of the man, he was compassionate and gifted with rare insight.

Jeri felt her skin prickle ominously. Nothing good could come of an attraction to a restless loner like Wade Evans. As Jerome had been, that kind of man had to be free to come and go with the seasons. Her mother had warned her. Loving Jerome O'Brian, she'd said, had been like trying to hold the wind.

And in so many ways, Wade Evans was very much like her father. Jeri reminded herself that she would do well to heed that long-ago warning.

Still, just remembering Wade's touch made Jeri's lips tingle and her face burn. So gentle. How could anyone so powerful have a touch so delicate, so elusive, so exciting?

Still, it was obvious that he resented her presence.

"Good grief," she muttered. How on earth did she expect him to feel? From his point of view, she'd come waltzing in, trying to take over his home—

She stood abruptly, roughly tossing her paint supplies back into the carrying case.

I have a right to be here, she told herself firmly, *and I'm not going to feel guilty.* Silently repeating this statement, Jeri mentally browbeat her psyche into submission. Jeri didn't want to take Wade's land. She only wanted to keep her father's legacy—to understand Jerome O'Brian's dream and to fulfill it.

"Do you hear that, Wade Evans?" she hollered into the trees. "I have a right to be here! Put that in your log and split it!"

Then she trudged toward the cabin, wondering why she hadn't noticed earlier that she had completely lost her mind.

She'd nearly reached the top of the knoll when she heard the crisp rustle of dry leaves punctuated by the snap of stepped-on twigs. Murphy bounded toward her, tongue lolling casually, obviously quite pleased to find her.

"Well, well." Jeri glared at the animal. "The wanderers return. Where's your boss?"

The tawny body circled her once, panting happily, then paced himself in front, leading her back toward the cabin.

"I appreciate the thought, dog, but I can make it back all by myself, and without the help of a four-footed escort."

Ignoring her black mood, Murphy happily tramped the path, stopping occasionally to sniff, scratch and perform other doggy functions. It was no surprise to see Wade's truck parked in the clearing. Where Murphy was, Wade was. Except at night. For some crazy reason the big Labrador had taken to sleeping at the foot of Jeri's bed, and she'd learned to leave her bedroom door slightly ajar so he could let himself in. Otherwise, the tenacious beast sat outside scratching until Jeri woke up and stumbled out of bed to open the door.

In the morning, truck, Wade and dog would all be gone.

From Jerome's letters, Jeri knew Wade had come to the valley to avoid a nine-to-five routine. Also, she'd noted the fact that Wade had been puttering at the cabin on a weekday afternoon when she'd arrived. One of these days, she would find out how he spent his time. But not today. Today she was in no mood for small talk.

Jeri stomped up the three steps onto the covered wood porch with more than the required amount of noise, then blasted through the front door dragging the awkward easel and case with one hand while trying to protect the freshly painted canvas she held in the other.

Appearing in the kitchen door, Wade watched her struggle with undisguised amusement. "Been painting?"

Roughly setting the case down, she managed to prop the easel against the wall and set the canvas on it to dry. She eyed Wade sullenly. He had no right to stand there looking that good.

"No," she snapped. "I've been scuba diving."

Wade's easy grin increased her consternation as he sauntered across the room to stand in front of her painting, examining it thoroughly.

"It's okay," he pronounced.

Jeri made a contemptuous sound. "You're too kind," she muttered, glaring at the annoying twinkle in Wade's eyes.

"A mite testy today, aren't we?" He was grinning broadly.

With an explicit but rather rude noise, Jeri turned and walked stiffly down the hall, wondering how Wade Evans would like to go through life with a paintbrush in his ear.

An hour later, Jeri had finished cleaning the creek mud from her body and headed out the kitchen door, blackberry bucket in hand. Wade looked up from his worktable, eyed the bucket and fixed her with a knowing grin. "Take care. Those bushes bite."

"I'll manage," she said crisply. "Unless, of course, you feel I should carry a weapon."

"Just a friendly warning. I'll go with you, if you want."

Jeri scowled. She was not in the mood to be patronized. "I'm sure a trek to the far side of the meadow is right up there with exploring the Amazon, but I think I can make it without an armed guide."

Wade shrugged and Jeri tightened her grip on the bucket handle as she spun and stalked away.

"Bring 'em back alive," he called, and Jeri fumed.

Her annoyance was short-lived as the beauty of the meadow captured her attention. The soft grass was slim-bladed and close-cropped, giving the look and feel of plush, jade-colored carpeting dotted randomly by yellow dandelion blooms.

The most virile of Gold Creek's blackberry bushes sprawled with thorn-covered viney branches, twisting among themselves until they stretched fully ten feet high. The cabin was still in sight, and Jeri was somewhat disappointed to note that Wade's attention had returned to the project on his workbench. Well, her mood was nothing that a huge batch of blackberry preserves couldn't improve, and she set to work.

Soon she was humming to herself, thoroughly enjoying the warmth of the day and her simple task. The bucket was nearly three-quarters full when she spotted a large cluster of absolutely immense berries about three feet above her reach. Using a dead branch, she tried to hook the vine and pull it down to her greedy grasp. The branch was mere inches too short.

With a frustrated grunt, she wedged her foot into the sturdy vee of the bush's thick trunk and hoisted herself up. Her moment of triumph was short-lived, for it was a brave vine, fighting valiantly to protect its juicy prize.

Jeri released the branch, assuming it would snap back up to its previous position. Instead, to her shock, the vine grabbed her by the shirt, sharp thorns impaling the fabric as the angry bush surrounded her.

"Oh, for pity sake... Ouch!" Each time she carefully grasped a thorn-free section and pulled, the movement caused an equal reaction behind her, and the barbed bush bit into her shirt.

Then disaster struck.

Her foot slipped and she plunged sideways into the spiny vine. With a choked cry, she threw her forearm across her eyes, and her hands thrust out to grasp at the vicious shrub, only to close around a palm full of stickers.

What a humiliating way to die. Eaten alive by a carnivorous blackberry bush. Oh, God.

Jeri was vaguely aware that the dog was barking wildly off in the distance, but the sound was overshadowed by the noise of her T-shirt being rent to shreds and the din of her own angry mutterings.

"Ow... Darn! Darn-darn-darn... Ow!"

The loud yelping was suddenly very close, and Jeri peeked out from under her arm to see Murphy peering into the bush, barking furiously. His nose was a mere two feet away, and she reached toward the animal as though he could actually do something to help her. Murphy continued to yip, but no way was he going to come into that bush after her.

Jeri didn't blame him one bit.

"Good grief, what in the world have you done to yourself now?" Wade took one look at Jeri's predicament and fought gallantly to suppress a smile. The situation wasn't funny, of course. But darned if she wasn't a sight.

Jeri saw Wade looming above her, and she flushed with embarrassment. "Is there any way you could help me out?" she asked in a voice that was deceptively cheerful.

He looked thoughtful. "Maybe. Wait there."

"Cute," Jeri replied in disgust as Wade trotted out of view. When he returned he was wearing thick leather gloves and carrying a pair of wicked-looking pruners.

"Hold tight," he muttered, and began a savage attack on the hapless bush. When Wade's arms slid down to lift her out of her barbed prison, it was the sweetest feeling on earth. He carried her across the meadow easily, as though she weighed no more than a dry leaf.

"Thank you," she mumbled against his shoulder, meaning it more than anything she had ever said in her life.

"Don't mention it," Wade replied pleasantly. He carried her into the cabin, releasing her reluctantly. She sat at the kitchen table feeling foolish. Her arms were thrashed, a road map of angry red scratches.

Wade frowned down at her. "Let's see those hands." Jeri meekly complied.

"You've got a dozen thorn heads in there," he pronounced, and promptly left the room, returning moments later with cotton, a bottle and a pair of tweezers. "Berry thorns are like poison. They'll fester if you leave them in." Wade reached for the antiseptic. "This may hurt a bit."

At the first sharp sting, Wade heard her gasp. What's more, he could almost feel her pain, like he'd experienced every danged thorn poke himself. She was so fragile. Small and delicate, trying so hard not to make a sound.

It made him want to pick her up and fight the world for her.

Good grief. What was happening to him, wanting to protect a stubborn, willful little she-cat who could probably shred a badger if she set her mind to it? He must be losing his mind.

He'd just spent three days trying to sort through the jumble of strange emotions that had been jerking his psyche around since Jeri O'Brian had waltzed into his life. He'd chopped enough wood to last his tenants all winter and repaired every loose nail on every house he owned in the valley. He'd spent so much time hanging around Ben's gas station that his old friend had finally tossed him out.

All this to avoid the temptation that now sat at his kitchen table. What did this woman want from him, anyway? Wade knew she had to want something. Women always did. He'd already decided that Jeri's fascination with Gold Creek had something to do with the source of its name—gold. What else could it be? She would be disappointed to discover that she couldn't just hopscotch along the creek picking nuggets like ripe berries, Wade told himself. When she learned that little lesson, Wade was certain she would beat feet back to the city.

Wade pulled his attention back to the task at hand, gently washing each wound with soothing antiseptic and using the tweezers to carefully pluck out the exposed thorns.

Jeri smiled up at Wade. "You should have been a doctor. You do good work."

He pulled out a chair and sat beside her, reaching out to gently stroke the back of his knuckle across a scrape on her cheek. "Poor baby. That soft, white skin of yours is all scratched up, isn't it?"

Jeri shrugged. "My own darn fault."

"That's true."

She tossed him a dry look. "Well, I probably shouldn't spoil you, but since you could've let me thrash around in that bush until I turned myself into confetti, I've decided to share."

"Share what?"

"I'm making blackberry pancakes."

"For dinner?" He shuddered at the thought.

"Certainly. Can't you picture thick pancakes, dripping with sweet butter and absolutely smothered with fresh blackberry preserves?"

Wade made a noise like a choked gurgle. "I'll pass."

"Nonsense." Jeri stood and gave him her sweetest smile. "You'll love them."

Wade stared into her soft, coppery eyes and decided that if she looked at him like that during dinner, he wouldn't know what he was eating anyway.

The woman was complicating his life.

After supper, Wade abruptly muttered something about catching the last of the daylight and disappeared outside to his worktable.

Jeri finished the dishes and was bleakly eyeing the purple-splotched sink, wondering if it would ever be white again, when Wade burst through the kitchen door with a triumphant grin. He reached toward a large, black paddle switch mounted near the doorway, flipping it to the On position, and was instantly rewarded by a loud coughing noise. Then there was a sputter, a rattle and a raucous pop followed by the low, vibrating hum of an engine sparking to life.

Listening blankly for a moment, Jeri was not certain exactly what monumental event had transpired, but instinctively realized that it had some obvious significance to Wade.

With the victorious flair of a conquering general, he marched across the room to flick a small vertical lever. Two long fluorescent ceiling bulbs blinked sleepily, then burst into glorious beacons.

"Ah, the generator." Jeri's gaze fixed on the brightly illuminated tubes.

"I fixed it." Wade's announcement was emphasized with a proud nod.

Willing herself to remain impassive, Jeri scrutinized first the glowing ceiling, then Wade's glowing face. "It's okay." She sauntered nonchalantly out of the room leaving a crestfallen craftsman in her wake.

Suddenly the steady hum became a sputter, coughing twice before dying to complete silence. The kitchen darkened to its previous forlorn dinginess, and Wade's forehead puckered in frustration. Jeri's audible snicker was met with a penetrating stare.

"Uh-oh," she sang, cheerfully grinning at his black scowl as he stomped toward the back door.

Shame on you Jeri O'Brian, she admonished herself, but the amused grin remained firmly glued on her lips, and she finally decided that Wade Evans could surely handle a bit of his own medicine.

Within five minutes the steady hum resumed, the kitchen was relit and Wade wandered sedately back into the living room. Jeri watched him closely, arching a delicate eyebrow in question.

He cleared his throat uneasily. "Out of gas," he mumbled, hastily heading down the hall to the lilting strains of Jeri's muffled laughter. It was soon drowned by the sound of water from the bathroom faucets being turned on full blast.

Still smiling, Jeri walked outside and stood on the porch to watch the pink-gold reflection of the setting sun dance across windswept clouds. The night was warm, the air heavy with nature's perfume of pine and sweet grass, and Jeri greedily gulped great lungfuls of the heady fragrance. When Wade came out, he had changed clothes, and a clean, soapy scent drifted toward her and mingled with the night bouquet.

Murphy bounded out of the house, passing Wade and jumping from porch to waiting truck in two massive leaps. He sat by the driver's door, tail swishing furiously in the soft dirt, impatiently waiting for Wade.

Jeri felt an inexplicable sense of depression settle across her like a cold, damp shroud.

"Going out?" she asked, knowing the answer even before the shaggy head gave an affirmative nod. They'd shared their first moments of nonhostile conversation today, and she'd begun to hope their relationship had reached a turning point. For some strange reason, she wanted to spend time with him, get to know more about the enigmatic Wade Evans. And she hoped he would want to know her better, as well.

Only as friends, of course.

They'd had such a nice time preparing dinner together, such an easy, comfortable rapport. It was as though they'd known each other for years. Jeri had mashed and simmered the berries into sweet, thick preserves, and Wade had drawn pancake duty. He'd informed her somewhat immodestly that he was an expert pancake flipper and had volunteered to teach her the proper pancake-flipping techniques.

The dog had especially enjoyed this lesson. Murphy had claimed several of the wayward cakes that had missed the pan and landed temptingly at his very paws.

Naturally, those had been carefully planned demonstrations of improper technique. A world-class flapjack flipper does not make such miscalculations, as Wade had haughtily informed Jeri.

Sighing audibly, Jeri turned and leaned on the porch rail. She truly hoped Wade wouldn't need another one of his disappearing acts now that they had made so much progress toward a more congenial relationship.

Besides, she was lonesome.

Not for Wade in particular, of course. Just for human company. Jeri's gaze settled on Murphy. Even nonhuman company would help.

"Could Murphy stay here?" she asked hopefully.

Wade was obviously surprised by her request. "That's up to him." At the sound of his name, the dog's head had cocked expectantly. "What about it, Murph? Want to keep the little lady company?"

The big Lab jumped up and ran toward the cabin, covering the distance from foot of steps to porch in a single vault. Leaping on Jeri, he placed one massive paw on each shoulder, causing her to stagger slightly backward against his weight. Before she could duck, Murphy covered her entire face with a juicy, tongue-dragging lick, then bolted back to the truck to resume his previous position.

Wade kept his face carefully impassive, but Jeri was infuriated by the amused sparkle in his eyes. Then his lips twitched, a minuscule movement, but she saw it and fumed silently.

"Sorry about that," Wade said, obviously not sorry at all. "Looks like it's the boys' night out."

"Take me with you." Her blurted entreaty was met by a dry chuckle.

"Not likely."

"Why not?" His expression tightened. Her tone softened. "Come on, Wade. I'd love to get out for a couple of hours and…" Her voice trailed off. And what? she thought frantically. Keep you in sight? Find out what in the devil you do every night? "And experience the valley's nightlife," she finished lamely.

Wade's raucous laughter assaulted her ears and flamed her face. "I don't think you'd exactly fit in with 'the valley's nightlife.'"

"How will I know unless I check it out? What would it hurt if you took me with you tonight?"

"Well," he said, drawing the word out. "You might crimp my style a bit."

Jeri didn't blink, but for some confusing reason her lungs seemed to tighten up a bit. "I will not. I promise to sit at a different table and pretend I don't even know you."

Wade bent over and picked up a small twig from the rough wood planks on the porch floor. He broke a small piece from the end of it, stared at it for a moment, then flicked it over the railing.

"What makes you think there are tables where I'm going?"

Stiffening, Jeri felt her stomach twist as the impact of his words settled there heavily. Resentment bubbled. "That's all the better." The words grated through clenched teeth. "Drop me off on your way to the brothel. Then you won't be around to put a crimp in *my* style."

Wade's eyes narrowed dangerously. "You can do anything you want, but I don't have to help."

His foot hit the last step before Jeri caught his arm to stop him.

"Please take me with you," she said. "I don't want to be alone tonight."

Wade searched her pale face, testing, measuring the depth of her unhappiness and finding mute reflection of his own misery. Turning away, he walked the final two steps and stood at the base of the porch, intently studying the twig in his hand and methodically cracking it into minute bits. He looked up at Jeri. She stood on the porch, backlit by a soft golden glow from the open cabin door, looking small, lost and vulnerable.

Wade was assaulted by an overwhelming urge. This was not the normal sexual yearning a man just naturally expected to feel for a good-looking woman. This was something new, something different. Something he'd never experienced before.

And he didn't much care for it.

It was an urge to protect her, keep her safe, away from the unpleasant realities of life. He didn't want her to discover things that would disappoint her, and if she stayed long enough, was persistent enough, she was bound to be hurt.

She didn't belong here, and Wade just had to keep reminding himself of that fact. He knew instinctively that this fragile creature threatened him in a way he couldn't identify. And Wade Evans was not a man to take kindly to threats.

By now the twig was completely shredded, and he dropped the pulpy remnants into the dust. The seed of an idea was germinating deep in the recesses of his mind, and he allowed it to grow until it blossomed into a full-fledged scheme. Maybe this was the opportunity he was looking for.

What if he *did* take her with him? What if he gave her a firsthand, up-close, face-to-face confrontation of rustic nightlife? Yes indeed, about thirty minutes at Happy Jack's Tavern ought to do the trick. That little outing should accomplish his goals nicely, set her back on those cute little heels and send her scampering for the nearest high rise. Back to the city. Back where she belonged.

Jaw set, eyes reflecting grim determination, Wade looked up into Jeri's anxious face.

"See to the generator," he snapped, then turned, long legs covering the distance to the truck before a stunned Jeri could fully comprehend the meaning of his terse statement. Wade yanked open the truck door, and Murphy leaped in. "Well? You coming or not?"

Jeri sprang into action.

"Wear shoes," Wade said dryly. "It's formal."

When the cabin was secure, she ran to the truck and climbed into the passenger seat. The dog, wedged between her and Wade, looked surprised but not displeased to see her join them. As the truck started down the dark dirt road to the main highway, Murphy put his big paws on Jeri's lap and with an "excuse me" look on his face, stretched his body across her to stick his face out the open window.

"You're in his seat."

Wade's remark was unnecessary. With a face full of dog, the extent of Jeri's reply was a muffled grunt. As they continued their trip in silence, Jeri stole a glance at Wade's determined face. Suddenly, she had a bad feeling about this.

A very bad feeling.

Chapter Four

The raucous noise emanating from their destination carried on the night breeze, reaching their ears a quarter mile before Jeri saw the small, dingy wooden building with a bright neon sign proclaiming Happy..beer..pool..Jack's.

As they pulled into the parking lot, the strains of Tammy Wynette standing by her man was all but drowned out by boisterous male laughter and an occasional shrill, coyote-like whoop. Jeri threw Wade a questioning glance.

"Valley nightlife," he mumbled, and got out of the truck, holding the door for Jeri. With a reluctant sigh, she slipped over the edge of the seat until her feet crunched on stone-and-glass-covered pavement. Wade locked the truck and moved quickly to the front door of the seedy-looking establishment. He said something to the dog that caused Murphy to circle twice and plop himself in a ball at the edge of the doorway.

Murphy's obviously on guard duty tonight, Jeri thought with irritation. Then she watched in horror as Wade disappeared into the peeling wooden structure, slamming the battered door behind him.

When she realized that Wade hadn't been kidding when he'd said he didn't want her hanging around to crimp his style, she began to seethe. "Well that's just fine with me." Jeri straightened her shoulders with a determined snap, marched to the door and grasped the rusty lever.

"Courage," she mumbled to herself as she pushed the handle down and pulled the heavy door open.

The exterior of the building was dingy, but the interior was positively alive, glowing brilliantly with the bright haze of refracted fluorescent light and cigarette smoke. Jeri blinked against the glare, adjusting her eyes to the tawdry dazzle. Neon colors bloomed in profusion, decorating every square inch of wall space by declaring It's Miller Time and pronouncing This Bud's for You.

Directly ahead of her was a long wooden bar, exactly the type John Wayne used to saunter up to, backed by the standard six-foot tavern mirror. A few well-worn, round tables were scattered around the right side of the room, and the entire left side was furnished with large green pool tables. The whole establishment was populated with noisy, very casually attired and somewhat scruffy-looking men.

And exactly three women, counting herself. One of her gender mates was skirting ribald remarks while balancing a tray of brown bottles over her head. The tray, along with the white apron she'd tied over her blue jeans, convinced Jeri that the lady was not here for fun.

The other woman was a mammoth, two hundred-pound-plus, heavily made-up blonde. Stiff white hair sprang from the woman's scalp as though attempting escape, and her torn leather ensemble would have made a Hell's Angel proud.

Scanning the room for Wade, Jeri saw that her presence was being duly noted by an uncomfortably large percentage of Happy Jack's customers. She shifted nervously. Wade may not want her hanging on him, but surely he wouldn't slip out the back and leave her here. Of course, he wouldn't.

If he did, she would bomb his generator, and no court in the county would convict her.

With a rush of relief, she recognized the broad back covered tightly by the blue-and-brown plaid Western-style shirt Wade was wearing. He was standing at the bar, one lean hip resting lightly against a plain, wooden bar stool. Jeri caught a movement from the corner of her eye and realized two very large, grinning human creatures were moving in her direction.

With as much self-assurance as she could muster, she stepped toward the bar, dodging the frazzled waitress and one small, spindly-legged old man, who was weaving erratically toward the door.

As Jeri sauntered up to the bar, a paunchy, T-shirted individual with a three-day growth of stubble stood behind the counter deftly flipping lids from bottles of assorted shapes. He gave a shrill whistle, and the waitress appeared, piled them on her tray and disappeared into the crowd. The bartender looked right over Jeri's head.

Okay, fine. Jeri deliberately placed herself three bar stools away from Wade. Far enough to give him some space, but close enough to give her some comfort.

The stubble-faced man saw Jeri and peered at her with small dark eyes. A toothpick was tightly clamped in his teeth, grooving in his lower lip and wiggling as he spoke.

"Want somethin'?" he asked with indifference.

"Yes, thank you. I'd like a wine cooler."

The small piggy eyes blinked once; the toothpick was momentarily motionless. He laid a meaty forearm on the bar and leaned toward Jeri until his face was a mere eighteen inches from hers.

"Come again?" His voice was disbelieving this time. And gruff.

Clearing her throat tensely, she repeated her request, and he straightened, staring at her bleakly. "Don't have that."

"Oh. Well, a glass of Chablis would be fine."

The bartender's eyes narrowed. "Sha-blee?"

Wade choked on his beer.

"I see." Jeri clamped her teeth together and spoke through them. "Exactly what *do* you have?"

"I got beer."

Wade tossed some money on the counter. Jeri could see he was thoroughly enjoying himself.

"Give the lady a beer, Jack." His grin was maddening. "After all, she wants to fit in."

Then Wade picked up his bottle and carried it into the crowd. He pulled up a chair, straddling it, joining a boisterous group of men who were obviously delighted to see him.

Happy Jack thunked an open beer bottle on the bar in front of Jeri.

"Uh...Mr.... Jack?"

The bartender gave an acknowledging grunt.

"May I please have a glass?"

"What the hell you need a glass for?" Jack bellowed.

Jeri's face began to flame as he—and half the bar—stared at her. She cleared her throat and spoke loudly enough to be heard by those interested. "Well, I'll tell you, Mr. Jack. Since I have to drink this unpalatable swill, I'd like to do it in a civilized manner."

Jack's eyes widened like two shiny beads, then narrowed dangerously. The small audience gathering around the scene went silent, except for the low hiss of a half-dozen sets of lungs expelling breath simultaneously. Jeri's stare was unflinching, but her stomach was break dancing under her liver, and she desperately hoped Wade would intervene if Mr. Jack decided to squeeze her like a ripe lemon.

Slowly Jack extended a beefy hand toward her, and Jeri willed her eyes not to waver. Then the beer bottle disappeared into his immense palm and, to her surprise, Jack rummaged beneath the counter and retrieved a tall glass. It was even clean.

He poured the foaming brew with a flourish, then set the glass gently in front of her.

"That what you had in mind, miss?" Jack's homely face was impassive, but there was a small glimmer of approval deep in his eyes.

She took a small sip, grimaced at the foul flavor, then tried to smile. "This is very nice. Thank you."

At this point, the uneasy silence surrounding them was broken by hoots and snickers. Someone hollered in a squeaky falsetto voice, "Hey, Jackie. How 'bout a glass for my beer?"

Happy Jack was not happy, and his stony stare hardened as he glared toward his tormentor. All snickering stopped, and the group began shuffling awkwardly, dispersing as they realized the show was definitely over. Jack looked back at Jeri. His mouth twitched slightly, and he winked at her.

"Just a pussycat at heart, aren't you?" whispered Jeri.

With a grimace that Jeri interpreted as a smile, Jack returned to his primary function of flipping bottle lids and whistling for pickup.

Jeri scrutinized the room and its diverse clientele. Three men seated at one of the tables were all grinning proudly at a tiny object that was being lavishly admired. The object seemed to be a small bottle, and Jeri knew instinctively that this was a group of miners showing off the fruits of their labor. They seemed as proud as first-time daddies. Strange, the effect that yellow stuff seemed to have on full-grown men.

"Hi there, sweetcheeks. Looking for company?"

A deep, slightly slurred masculine voice interrupted her thoughts, and Jeri turned to see an immense, furry-faced man with a ragged thatch of dirty blond hair. A second man, much smaller but just as grimy, stood behind him. The shorter man had a huge scar splitting his face from forehead to jaw, separating one black eyebrow into two bushy splotches and leaving a jagged white tear through his dark beard. Both men were scruffy, unwashed and unpleasantly scented. They leered drunkenly.

"You new around here, honey?" The blond man moved between Jeri and the table of miners, effectively blocking them and half the room from her view. She found herself staring at a large, sweaty chest, bare but for the sleeveless denim vest draped across him like a tattered shroud.

Annoyed by their intrusion, Jeri glared up at him, hoping an indignant expression would convey her displeasure and hasten their retreat. Instead, she felt her own body stiffen, shuddering at the hard glint of the big man's squinting eyes. A lewd smirk twisted his lips. Jeri forced her gaze to remain level; his question remained unanswered.

His eyes narrowed even further as he propped himself casually against the bar. "Name's Stud, honey," he told her, with rather proud emphasis. Leaning closer, his mouth braided into a grimace. "Can you guess why?"

The man smelled of stale beer, stale tobacco and stale sweat. Jeri's nose wrinkled. "Because you have the IQ of a two-by-four, I imagine."

Stud shot Jeri a venomous look, then his lips twisted. "Sassy little piece, ain't you?" He eyed the deep scratch across her cheek. "But that's okay. Always did like a woman with spirit. Kinda' spices things up."

With a lecherous grin, Stud pulled up a stool and sat next to her, reopening her view of the room. A quick glance confirmed that Wade was watching carefully. Jeri felt an enormous sense of relief. One of the three miners was watching, too, a small, wiry and seemingly benign man with large, owlish eyes. Jeri thought she detected a look of concern on his face as Stud's scraggly companion took up guard duty on her other side, effectively roping her off from the outside world.

"This here's Bearmeat," Stud said, waving a gangly hand in his friend's general direction. Bearmeat smirked, stared at Jeri's chest and nodded. His dark eyes glittered. "We do timbering 'tween here and Fort Jones."

"How nice for you," Jeri mumbled, her eyes riveted on the friendly miner's face. He was quietly signaling for her to join them, and Jeri slipped off the bar stool. "If you'll excuse me—" Her exit speech was interrupted as Stud's heavy arm dropped in front of her like a railroad-crossing gate.

"If you're looking for a good time, honey, we sure can give it to you." Stud grinned, revealing a row of tiny, chipped teeth the same dirty-yellow color as his hair, and Bearmeat emitted a high-pitched giggle.

Jeri gave Stud a blank stare, pretending not to grasp the meaning of his lewd remark. Her lack of reaction seemed to have the desired effect as the big man's eyes glazed slightly and his lips sagged. He dropped his arm, quickly standing in front of Jeri, leaning so close that his odor made her gag. Clamping his hands on the bar behind her, he pinned her between two bulky arms. "Come on, baby. Be nice."

Bearmeat licked his lips, hiccupped and giggled again.

"The only thing you could possibly give me," she said frostily, "is a renewed appreciation of underarm deodorant."

Stud straightened in surprise, dropping his hands to his side. His furrowed brow indicated that he knew he'd been insulted; the blank look in his eyes assured Jeri he couldn't quite figure out how.

Taking advantage of his momentary confusion, she slipped between the two lumberjacks and made a beeline toward the owl-eyed miner.

The small, friendly-faced man had been watching developments carefully. He stood quickly, pulling out a chair for her. Jeri sank into it gratefully.

The miners were watching the bar carefully, as though daring Stud and Bearmeat to follow. When the three men relaxed in their chairs, leaning back casually and smiling pleasantly at her, she knew the loggers had given up.

"Thank you," she murmured nervously, hoping she hadn't jumped into the proverbial fire. Wade was close by, though. Probably enjoying her discomfort immensely, too, but Jeri knew he would be there if she really needed him.

He would never let her forget it, either.

Smiling tentatively, Jeri introduced herself to her table-mates.

"Glad to meet you, Miss O'Brian. I'm Nathan Loomis and this ugly devil is Buck Mankin...." Loomis motioned to a large, middle-aged man across the table. Buck responded with a gap-toothed grin and extended his hand, engulfing Jeri's as he gave it a powerful shake.

"The young 'un there is Tad Sumner," Loomis continued, and Jeri smiled into a bashful, teenaged face. Tad mumbled something incoherent as he intently studied the battered wood surface of the table.

"Nice to meet you, Tad," Jeri said warmly. Tad's Adam's apple bounced nervously, and he blushed to the roots of his crew cut.

This group seemed blessed with honest-to-goodness human manners, and Jeri began to relax. Nathan Loomis seemed to perceive her thoughts.

"You're safe now, Miss O'Brian," he said. "Most loggers are okay, but those two are snake mean. They won't bother you while you're with us."

"Please call me Jeri," she said. "I can't thank you enough for coming to my rescue. You're miners, aren't you?"

Loomis laughed good-naturedly. "Well, there's some that would argue that, but we like to think so."

"My father was a miner. He had a claim up on Gold Creek. Do you know it?"

Loomis looked thoughtful. "I've heard of it. Never worked it, though."

"We're from Washington. Olympia," Buck added. "We only get down here for the season."

"The season?"

"Dredging season. June through September."

"Oh." Jeri thought for a moment. "Dredge. My father wrote about a dredge. Said he and Wa—his partner built one. What do dredges do?"

"They're like big, floating vacuum cleaners," Buck explained. "They suck up the bottom of the river, then throw the gravel over a sluice and the gold drops out."

Jeri's eyes widened. "Really? Have you found much gold?"

Nathan and Buck beamed proudly and Tad grinned sheepishly as Loomis dug into the pocket of his worn work shirt, pulling out a familiar glass vial. Inside was a single nugget, slightly flattened on one side, about the size of a fat corn flake.

Jeri caught her breath. "It's beautiful. You found this?"

"Yep. It's a nice little nugget." He leaned forward, lowering his voice to a conspiratorial whisper. "We've pulled out about ten ounces since June, but this is the biggest piece."

"So far," added Buck optimistically. "We're finally at bedrock. We might find more."

"Where's your claim," Jeri asked, "or is it a secret? I don't mean to pry."

"It's right on the river, about fifty yards south of Walker Bridge," Buck said. "It's no secret. Anyone driving down Highway 96 can see us working."

"Hey, Loomis." They looked simultaneously toward the pool-hall section of the bar where a burly man was circling his hand over his head in a signal. "Your table, boys," he called.

Nathan stood. "It's our turn. Care to join us, miss?"

"I haven't played in years." Jeri smiled. "But I used to be fair."

"Partners, then. You and me'll whip the tar out of these two," Nathan said, with a wink at Jeri and a puffy grin at his friends.

Buck laughed. "The devil, you say. Let's see the color of your money, Nat." Mankin flashed a five-dollar bill.

"I hope you can afford to lose that," Loomis said. "Because it's as good as mine."

Of the four pool tables crowded in the area, one stood empty, and Buck promptly tossed a triangular-shaped object onto the green felt surface. He and Tad began tossing the multi-hued wooden balls into the form until it was filled. With loving care, Buck vibrated the pack of balls until he was satisfied, then removed the mold to leave a perfectly formed set.

"My break." Nat grabbed a cue stick from the wall rack.

Loomis made a good break, calling stripes and sinking two more shots before missing a third. The miss was greeted by good-natured hoots from his companions and a sympathetic nod from Jeri. While Buck angled and measured his shots like the Klamath Valley version of Minnesota Fats, Jeri glanced at Wade and was surprised to see him watching her openly. His expression was muted, but his eyes sparkled with amusement.

Jeri frowned at him. She was not a fool and had already ascertained that Wade's choice of establishment tonight had not been made with her enjoyment in mind. She also had a pretty fair idea of his motive. Well, she certainly wouldn't be running out the door, whimpering and wailing. If Wade was looking for her to supply his evening's entertainment, she would at least have the choice of scripts.

"Okay, Jeri. Go for it."

"Pardon me?" Jeri blinked at Nathan, who was grinning at her, his huge eyes shining. He thrust out a stick nearly as long as Jeri was tall. She took it tentatively.

"My turn already?" A quick glance at Buck's glum face and the arrangement of solid balls on the table conveyed the fact that Mankin had not performed up to his own expectations.

Jeri was nervous. Just about every eye in the bar was on her, and she hadn't played pool since she was fourteen. She'd been pretty good at it then, though. Jerome O'Brian was a fine teacher, and her lessons had been at establishments that made this one seem like the Hilton.

Still, it had been a lot of years ago.

With determination, Jeri slowly circled the table, eyeing the setup. Fortunately, her newly-found friends were no great shakes with the stick, either. Buck had left her an easy corner shot, and mentally, she was setting the table several shots ahead.

Leaning across the long end of the table, Jeri felt awkward and rusty, but she easily popped the violet-striped ball into the corner. Holding her breath, she watched the white cue ball roll back toward center table almost, but not quite far enough to line a sure second shot.

Rats. Jerome wouldn't have been pleased.

As she was sizing up her chances, a familiar unpleasant aroma assailed her nostrils, and small hairs bristled on her nape.

"Regular little hustler, ain't you?" Stud whispered from behind her. "Need some help?"

Jeri felt his chest brush her back as his arms started to circle her, and she was engulfed by a wave of nausea and repugnance.

Teeth clamped, Jeri's voice dropped to a savage whisper. "Don't touch me with any part of your body you plan to use again," she warned.

The hairy arms froze in midair, then withdrew as Stud let out a surprised laugh. Jeri felt a muggy breeze tickle her back and knew he'd stepped away. But he was still close. Too close.

Trying to ignore him, she willed her mind back to the angle of her shot. When she decided on a strike point, she leaned over, positioning the cue stick alongside the length of her torso.

Suddenly, she felt a hard body pressing against her bottom. Stud began to lower his chest over her back to pin her to the table, and Jeri panicked. She could feel his breath rasp against her neck.

Jeri jammed the cue stick backward, satisfied as Stud's breath left him with a single gurgled whoosh. He doubled over and slid to his knees, arms folded around his midsection, eyes wild, mouth gaping like a beached fish.

"I'm so sorry," Jeri said sweetly. "Why, I had no idea you'd be standing so close while I was shooting."

Stud's mouth continued its soundless flapping, and a quick movement caught Jeri's attention. Bearmeat's face was contorted with rage as he stepped forward menacingly. He held something, waving it with small circles and jabbing movements. A low guttural sound bubbled from his throat.

Jeri saw the glint of the knife blade at the same moment the familiar blue-and-brown plaid appeared in front of her. Wade's back was toward her, but he reached behind to grasp her wrist.

"Go on to the truck," Wade said, tossing her the keys and giving her a gentle nudge toward the front door. Jeri took a step, then hesitated. How could she leave Wade here to fight a crazed maniac with a knife? Stud was beginning to get his breath back; then there would be two of them.

This was all her fault. She couldn't leave Wade. Empty beer bottles seemed to adorn every ledge and perch in the room, and Jeri grabbed one, using the neck of the bottle as a handle. She had absolutely no idea what she was going to do with it; she only knew if anyone tried to hurt Wade, she would use it.

While Bearmeat snarled at Wade, Buck Mankin quietly flanked him. With a deft movement, Buck reached around and grabbed the smaller man's wrist, twisting it until the knife clattered to the floor. Casually, Mankin bent down to retrieve the weapon, keeping a firm fistful of Bearmeat's shirt.

Still lying on the floor, Stud stopped thrashing and glared up at Wade. Stud's hand was slowly slipping into the pocket of his jeans when Wade set a booted foot on his chest.

"I wouldn't do that." Wade glanced toward Jeri. "Get in the truck," he told her firmly. "Now."

Jeri put the bottle down and began to back toward the door. Nathan Loomis grinned at her, giving Jeri a quick wink before he and two other men began to haul Stud to his feet. Then Jeri pushed open the heavy door, almost tripping over Murphy in her haste, and ran for the relative safety of the truck.

The night air flowed through the open windows as the truck wound the dirt road toward the cabin. Jeri was in the middle of the bench seat, having relinquished the window position to Murphy. Wade was watching the road, his lips pursed thoughtfully, appearing unaware of Jeri's presence mere inches from him.

He was, in fact, intensely aware of her.

Jeri cleared her throat. "I suppose I should thank you for your help—"

"No need," Wade interrupted. The truck lurched slightly as the left tire hit a rut, and Jeri bounced against Wade's hard torso. She straightened quickly, steadying herself by grabbing the dashboard. Wade's arm and shoulder tingled from the brief contact.

"You'd better learn to stifle your tongue, though," Wade said. "You keep baiting roughnecks like that, and you'll need an armed escort just to buy groceries."

He saw a crimson flush creep across her cheek. "I wouldn't normally find myself in that situation. Happy Jack's was not my idea."

Wade threw her a questioning glance. "No?"

"Well, I admit I asked you to take me with you." She eyed him warily. "But I certainly didn't think you were going anywhere so...so—"

"Rustic?"

Jeri folded her arms and grunted in frustration. "You are the most irritating, the most aggravating, the most exasperating man I've ever met."

Wade looked pleased.

The truck groaned up the final grade and Wade steered into the clearing in front of the cabin. Wade got out, but Jeri didn't move fast enough to suit Murphy, who simply leaped over her to exit out Wade's door with an excited yelp, hitting the soft dirt on all four paws. Wade could hear Jeri mutter to herself as she climbed out.

"I know exactly why you took me there, Wade Evans. You're trying to chase me away."

Wade was already on the porch. He turned and stared at the fiery creature stomping toward him. "You don't belong here."

"That's your opinion."

"Yep."

Wade went into the cabin. The evening hadn't turned out as he'd planned. He'd expected Jeri to faint when she'd seen Happy Jack's rather unsavory establishment. Instead, she'd had Jack himself eating out of her hand and had half the bar cheering her on. No, that was definitely not what he'd had in mind.

"Wade?"

"Umm?"

"Did you and my father have a dredge?"

At her question, Wade froze, standing motionless in the doorway for several seconds before he continued into the kitchen and turned on the generator. He'd dreaded this moment from the day she tripped up that damned road but he still didn't know how to handle it.

He walked to the refrigerator and opened the door. "Want a sandwich?" he mumbled in a tone that indicated he couldn't care less whether she wanted one or not.

She sure didn't waste time, Wade thought. She's already learning how to pull gold out of the creek, and it's just a question of time before she learns a whole lot more. The thought made him feel sick.

Jeri joined him in the kitchen, smiling at the array of lunch meat and cheese spread on the table. "I'm not hungry. Wade? Did you have a dredge?"

Persistent little devil, Wade thought irritably, but he knew she would keep at him until she got her answer. "Yes."

"Where is it?"

Ignoring the question, Wade finished spreading a liberal coating of mayonnaise on a slice of bread, then piled a half-inch-thick assortment of fillings on it. To Jeri's obvious consternation, he cleaned off the table, took a bite of the sandwich and walked into the living room without even acknowledging her question.

She followed, and Wade knew she was watching him sullenly. When he had finished his sandwich, she walked around to the couch where he was sitting and planted herself in front of him, arms crossed.

"Well?"

Wade looked up at her, trying to maintain an impassive expression. His voice was tinged with sadness. "Why do you want to know?"

"Because I want to try it. It's something my father loved to do, and I want to try it."

She sat next to him, face lighting with excitement as she touched his arm in a pleading gesture. "Show me how to use it, Wade. Please?'

The tight clamp of his jaw gave her the answer even before he shook his head. "No," he said resolutely, and stood. Jeri emulated him, dogging his movements as he tried to walk toward the hall.

"Why not?"

"It's dangerous." Wade's tone left no room for argument.

"Dangerous? It's dangerous to drive on a freeway." Jeri was frustrated. "Why does every conversation with you turn into a giant argument? Dangerous or not, it's half mine, and I'm going to learn how to use it."

Wade looked at her thoughtfully. "You've got to find it first."

Defeated momentarily, Jeri's shoulders slumped. She looked too tired to argue, but Wade had no illusions that she was going to give up. Apparently, however, she'd decided that this wasn't the time to deal with the dredge issue.

Wade looked down at her, noting the dejected droop of her head. Of its own accord his hand came up, lightly stroking soft brown curls before cupping her chin to tilt her face back. She sure was a spitfire, he thought. She led with her chin, just like her pa. He would have been proud of her tonight. She'd stood her ground.

Wade smiled at the mental picture of Jeri standing in that seedy bar holding a grimy beer bottle like a club. A five-foot-nothing scrub of a woman trying to protect him from two crazy lumberjacks with a stupid bottle. She'd been like a mama bear with cubs.

Jeri had more courage than sense, Wade decided, but danged if she wasn't beautiful. He saw her eyes widen under his intense scrutiny, reflecting a soft amber glow. Her lips were moist, full, hypnotizing.

Wade bent his head lower, his gaze locked into the luminous coppery depths. She raised her chin slightly, her lips parting in soft, unconscious invitation. He'd wanted those lips since the first day he'd seen her, and here she was, eyes half closed, that sweet mouth raised toward him, quivering, just begging him to taste her.

The alarm in his brain sounded again and again and again, but this time Wade wasn't listening.

Jeri held her breath, her eyes riveted to the firm, molded lips hovering inches above her own. Don't turn away from me, she pleaded silently, even as she steeled herself for rejection. As she felt his arm slide around her waist, she tensed, afraid even a blink might break the spell. Then suddenly she knew, she realized with a sweet certainty that Wade wasn't going to turn away.

Wade was going to kiss her. Finally.

Chapter Five

The realization sent a shiver of anticipation through Jeri's body, weakening her knees and numbing her feet. Her fingertips rested against his chest, as much to feel the hard sinew as to prop her own failing limbs. Her palms absorbed his heat. Each pounding thud of his heart sent a palpitating message to her own, until both heartbeats seemed to pulse in unison.

His lips came closer, slowly lowering until they lightly brushed the corner of her mouth, as though sipping the nectar of her skin. "Sweet thing," he murmured. "You feel so good in my arms."

Careful, Jeri, her mind screamed. *Dangerous territory here.* But it was too late for caution, and she knew it.

Jeri felt her entire body trembling as she sagged against him. She hesitated, unsure, then slid her fingers up his chest and across the hard ridge of his collarbone.

Softly, gently, Wade's lips brushed across hers. He kissed her eyelids, her cheeks, then fitted his mouth over hers with exquisite care, moving his lips until hers parted, then moaning his pleasure. Jeri had been kissed before, but never with such reverence, such awe. A deep warmth pulsed from her scalp to her toes.

She felt him shudder. The kiss ended, and she felt a poignant sense of loss. Of their own accord, her fingers locked behind his neck, urging him closer.

When Wade took her mouth again, it was hot, hard and demanding, possessing her powerfully, completely. The room seemed to spin as sharp shocks jolted her. He encircled her in his arms, tightening, pressing her against him.

Deep inside her, sweetness mingled with need, an intense desire for this man and this man only. Jeri returned his kisses with a desperate longing far beyond the depth of her experience.

She whimpered, a soft, throaty sound that turned into a husky moan of pleasure. His lips burned a trail down her throat. "Wade," she murmured, repeating his name again and again. She felt soft tremors racking him with each whispered word.

Then he stiffened and pulled back. He swore, a quiet, ragged oath of despair, and turned away from her.

Confused, Jeri reached out. He stood, as though paralyzed. "Don't," he said.

Her hand froze. "What is it? What's wrong?"

He stood silently, his back to her, until his breath lost its ragged edge. "I shouldn't have done that," he said finally.

"Why?" Jeri was hurt and bewildered by Wade's rejection. "It was something we both wanted."

"You're like a small bird, all wide-eyed and trembling. You're alone and vulnerable, and if your daddy was here, he'd have my hide for what I'm thinking."

"What has my father got to do with this? Good grief, I'm not a child, and my father hasn't cared what I did or with whom for years."

"That's where you're wrong, honey." Wade faced her. He looked tired and tense. "He cared a lot, and it flat tore him up to know he couldn't be there for you."

"Couldn't? I think you mean *wouldn't*." She felt her chest begin to tighten and ache. "It was his choice."

Wade sighed. "Maybe, maybe not."

"What do you mean by that?"

"I mean, there may be things you don't know." His tone was gruff, as though he hadn't wanted to get into this discussion with her.

"What things?"

"Just *things*." He made a noise, giving vent to his frustration. "Kids don't always know what's going on, that's all. It's late. Go to bed."

"No. Wade—"

"Forget it." He turned and strode into the kitchen.

She followed. "Why do you always do this?"

"Do what?"

"Turn away from me. I like you, Wade." Her voice was suddenly shy. "Heaven only knows why, but I do." Wade stopped. Jeri continued to talk to his back. "Sometimes I think you...like me, too, but then you pull back and get angry, and I, well, I just don't understand any of it. What's wrong with me, anyway?"

When Wade faced her, he was once more in control, his expression impassive. "Nothing's wrong with you. You know what you want and you're going after it. I'm just not going to roll over and give it to you."

Staring in disbelief, Jeri paled, her eyes cavernous orbs in her pinched, white face. "What are you saying?"

"You know exactly what I'm saying, honey. Nice try."

Trembling, Jeri's eyes anchored on Wade's face. She was shocked. Someone had hurt him, she realized suddenly, had hurt him badly. She had been so wrapped up in her own pain that she'd been blind to the fact that Wade, too, was suffering.

"I don't want anything from you, Wade," she said softly. "Except your friendship."

Wade's eyes snapped at the unexpected statement, at the softness of her voice. He saw pity in her eyes, and his insides seemed to explode. He quickly turned away, hoping to hide his pain.

When he finally spoke, his tone was calm, controlled. Emotionless. "So you want nothing from me? Nothing at all?"

Jeri's heart froze at the obvious answer. Gold Creek. Wade thought she wanted Gold Creek. The land represented her father's dream, who Jerome O'Brian was as a man and who she was as his daughter.

So, in a sense, Wade was right.

Flecks of dawn light dappled the creek, and shimmering cascades broke over boulders nested in the belly of the stream.

Jeri watched the white foam crash into rock, twisting and swirling in a powerful vortex then plunging over the stony precipice. At the waterfall's base, the creek relaxed, languishing in the quiet serenity of a deep green pool. Like all living things, Gold Creek was a complex, conflicting panorama, powerful yet fragile, both gentle and cruel.

Shivering, she pulled her white windbreaker more tightly around her chest, then sought out a large, sun-warmed rock. Even summer days were cool in the heavy shade of the creek's trees. Jeri had been here since before dawn, taking comfort in the drone of rapids, the rustle of spring leaves.

Even the solace of the water couldn't ease the tormented ache of her mind. Why had she really come to Gold Creek? What giant hand had pushed her to this valley, holding her against the meadow's bosom like a starving child at its mother's breast?

Jeri flushed remembering Wade's accusations last night. It was partly her fault, she realized. She'd been subtly sending signals since the first day she'd seen him. That first day, when a man as big as a mountain had looked at her with eyes mirroring the blue of the sky and the green of spring grass at the same time. It was as though she'd never seen a man—any man—before.

A cracking twig broke her thoughts, and a moment later Murphy bounded into the clearing with a wet, exuberant greeting.

From a nearby ridge, Wade watched silently, then stepped into view, feigning surprise at Jeri's presence. "What are you doing here?"

The attempt failed miserably. He knew by the responding arch of her eyebrow that she realized he'd been looking for her.

She had the grace not to call him on it. "I like it here," she said softly. "It's beautiful."

Wade nodded and tossed a pebble into the creek. "Sun's barely up." He shifted uncomfortably, remembering his momentary sense of panic when he'd found her room empty this morning, and he still wondered at the shattering, gut-wrenching feeling of loss he'd felt. "I thought maybe you were painting." A lie. He'd seen her easel in the living room. "Nice morning for a walk." Sure. She didn't answer.

"About last night..." Wade began, then cleared his throat. "I was out of line."

"When?" Her voice was soft, cool, expressing a calmness she didn't feel. "When you kissed me, or when you insinuated I was trying to trade my body for the land?"

He winced. "I had no right to do either. Your daddy'd string me up for treating you like that." He flung another rock into the water. "You didn't deserve it."

She couldn't meet his eyes. "It was as much my fault as yours. You're a very, ah, attractive man, and I guess I've been, well, a bit lonely."

Wade nodded as though she hadn't just stabbed him in the chest with her words. Lonely. Of course, that was it. They were both just lonely.

"We have a rather complicated situation," she said. "Your presence here threw a monkey wrench into my plans, and I've invaded your privacy, haven't I?"

"We're partners and that's a fact." He shrugged. "Doesn't much matter whether we like it or not. It's something we've got to work out."

"How are we going to do that?"

"Will you sell out to me?"

"No!" Her eyes flashed. "This land was my father's dream. It's all I've got left of him."

Wade sighed. He'd expected that. What he hadn't expected was the relief he felt at her answer. "So what are you going to do?" he asked quietly.

"I don't know." She made an impatient noise. "It seems I never know what to do until it's too late." Jeri stood and walked to the edge of the creek, staring down at her own reflection, distorted in the swirling water. "Last winter, Daddy wanted me to come back here with him, but I wanted to think about it. I was still thinking a month later, and he was gone."

"That wasn't your fault, honey." God, no. It was my fault, Wade told himself, my fault you lost your daddy right when you should have been finding him. How would she feel when she found out what *really* happened to Jerome O'Brian?

"I just...didn't trust him." Jeri looked at Wade with wide, pain-filled eyes. "After all those years, I couldn't bring myself to believe he suddenly wanted me again."

Wade couldn't bear to watch her suffer. It wasn't his place to tell her, but how could he just stand by and let her hurt like that? "Honey, he always wanted you. He just couldn't tell you so."

"You keep saying that word—*couldn't*. He walked out on his own two feet."

"That he did, but maybe someone told him to."

"Who?" Jeri whispered, obviously shocked. "My mother? Are you saying that my mother told him to leave?"

Wade was irritated with himself. He knew he should've kept his mouth shut, but he was in too deep to extricate himself easily. "What did she tell you about it?"

Jeri's eyes clouded as she traveled a mental time path. "She told me he wouldn't be back." And Margaret O'Brian's voice had been as cold as death, Jeri remembered. "She told me that loving a man like Jerome O'Brian was like trying to hold the wind. The harder you try to grab it, the faster it slips away." Jeri could see her mother's eyes, empty and haunted as she'd refused to comfort her only child, withdrawing instead into her own shell of misery. "My mother loved him. She couldn't have kicked him out." Jeri whirled, eyes wet and angry. "You're lying!"

Wade went to her then, cupping her head in one big palm, pulling her face to his chest. Stroking her hair, Wade murmured softly to her. "I'm sorry, honey. It's just that you need to know that he cared about you. Your mama loved you, too, but she needed things. Jerome needed dreams."

Things. Straightening, Jeri wiped at her face. Her mother *did* need things. "But she loved my father. I could see it, feel it." Her mind brought forth other images, unpleasant memories Jeri had chosen to ignore. "He was always chasing those dreams, always leaving us alone. Mother resented him for that." Startled, Jeri stared up. "I remember her anger. Somehow, I'd forgotten..." Forgotten the fancy condo, fast cars, fast friends, fast track. But somewhere along the way Margaret O'Brian had gotten it all and lost it all. She had died young and alone, confusing acquaintances for friends, leaving a daughter she hardly knew and a man who'd loved her quietly, with the desperate despair of knowing he could never make her happy.

Stiffly, Jeri pulled away from the comfort of Wade's arms. "I—I think I'd like to be alone now. Please."

Wade hesitated, then asked, "You okay?"

Nodding, she forced a smile. "Yes, I'm fine."

Wade appeared unconvinced, but respected her request. Jeri watched him disappear over the ridge, then her thoughts returned to her parents.

Jeri was part of them both. She had her father's stubborn determination and love of nature, yet she was inwardly a frightened, solitary creature like her mother. So many contradictions, such a bloody war of conflict battling in one small body.

Jeri felt so helpless, so weak.

Confusion circled her like a sworn enemy, one she couldn't seem to defeat and didn't know how to fight. She'd turned her back on her rootless childhood and her mother's life-style, choosing instead to follow her father's vision. If she gave up Gold Creek, the only gift her father had had to give would be gone forever. If she fought for it and won, somehow she knew she would be taking the only thing Wade really loved, and it might destroy him.

"No...no." The soft whimper was lost in the roar of the creek as cool spray misted her face, mingling with salty tears of torment. "Oh, Daddy," she sobbed. "I don't know what I should do. Oh, God, how I wish I knew what you wanted me to do."

The sun had climbed hotly into the midmorning sky before Jeri returned to the cabin and saw Wade loading split wood into the back of the beleaguered pickup truck.

He looked up, stopping only briefly before grasping another log with gloved hands and tossing it onto the pile already in the truck bed.

"Car's ready," he said.

Jeri blinked at him in confusion.

"Ben called. Your car's ready."

"Oh. That's . . . good."

For some strange reason Jeri didn't feel the news was particularly good at all, but she couldn't understand why. Since her abused brain seemed to be the consistency of cold oatmeal, however, she had no desire to further analyze any obscure psychological implications.

"Will he be bringing it here?"

Wade's smile twisted. "Not likely. We'll have to pick it up."

Jeri nodded. "Of course."

The last of the wood landed roughly on top of the pile, and Wade snapped the tailgate into position. "I've got a stop to make first, then I'll take you up to Ben's if you want."

"I'd appreciate that," Jeri said. "If you have a couple of minutes, I'd like to wash up first."

"Don't take all morning. And put on some shoes." He'd noticed her tearstained face and red eyes underlined with dark shadows, and he felt a sharp stab of indefinable emotion as he watched her walk to the cabin. Wade felt guilty, as though he'd caused her pain by telling her the truth about her parents. Maybe he should have kept his mouth shut, he thought, but it wasn't his fault she'd had a materialistic mother and an irresponsible father. Blast it all. A woman like Jeri deserved better.

Instinctively, Wade knew this woman was unique, special and, to him anyway, dangerous.

Jeri returned, washed but still withdrawn and quiet. Soon the truck was winding along the dirt road toward the main highway. Murphy, having commandeered the window seat, left Jeri sitting rigidly beside Wade, curling her fingers stiffly around the edge of the seat cushion to keep from brushing against him during the rugged ride.

Wade looked grimly toward Jeri. Her face was pale, bloodless, and her eyes had clouded to a lifeless dusty brown.

Jeri shifted against the hard bench seat of the pickup. "It'll be good to have my car back. I'll stop at the post office on the way back and ship my paintings off."

"Where're you sending them?"

"To a gallery in San Francisco. They've been handling my work for years."

Wade's head bobbed toward the parcels stowed behind the seat. "Are your paintings any good?"

Jeri managed a smile. "I hope so. I think they're some of the best work I've done." Her tone turned serious. "I just hope they're salable. At this point, I can't afford the luxury of pure creative license."

When she fell into a brooding silence, Wade asked, "You okay?"

"Umm? Oh, yes, I'm fine, and I want to thank you."

"What for?"

"For telling me something difficult, something you thought I should know."

Wade made a noncommittal sound. "It seems to have made things worse for you."

"No, not really. You just reminded me of some things I'd tried to forget." She reached over and laid her fingers on Wade's arm. "But you also showed me that I wasn't the cause of my parents' failure, and I thank you for that. I guess I was surprised that you knew so much about us...about my mother."

"Men talk." Shifting uncomfortably, Wade angled the big truck onto the highway. "Jerome and I had a bit in common there."

"Oh?"

"My wife was a lot like your mama. She liked money, wanted the good life."

Jeri looked out the window. "This *is* the good life."

With a dry laugh, Wade said, "Not to Marnie. She was a city girl...." His gaze washed over Jeri. "She liked money, and I had a lot of it then." Wade's mind wandered. Yes, he'd had it all, money and power. He'd been ruthless in their pursuit. Wade had taken the city by storm, determined never again to be cold or hungry or poor. Land was power, and he'd bought all he could get; apartment complexes, industrial buildings, raw acreage—all of it. Although his holdings had been substantially depleted, the remnants of his empire allowed Wade to enjoy his current unhurried lifestyle.

"What happened?" Jeri asked.

"Guess I'm a soft touch." That's what his accountant had said, anyway. When Wade had begun to see the misery beneath his empire, the human suffering of those struggling to pay the price of living in his concrete monuments, he'd tried to change things. Lowering rents until his banker had screamed in anguish, his own cash reserves had soon become dangerously depleted.

"When the money went, she went," Wade said.

"That must have hurt you."

"No." Surprised, Wade realized that it hadn't really hurt at all. "I was relieved. It was my fault, anyway."

"I doubt that. It usually takes two people to make a relationship and two people to break one."

"Not in this case. Marnie was honest about what she wanted from me. I changed, she didn't." That was true, Wade acknowledged. His wife had seen her own life-style, her security, everything she'd married Wade to acquire, slipping away. Finally in desperation and while there were still some assets to retrieve, she'd divorced him, then built a veritable fortune on the ashes of Wade's evicted tenants.

The marriage had lasted less than two years, but the lessons gleaned from it still haunted him. If his wife had been honest about what she'd been after, however, Denise hadn't been, and the remembrance of that second and ultimate failure had hardened him for good.

Jeri watched Wade's face tighten, his jaw set. She saw the pain and determination in his eyes and wondered how any woman could reject a man like Wade Evans.

Before she could say anything further, Wade slowed the truck and turned into a small, private driveway that hairpinned twice before stopping in front of a charming, gingerbreadlike house.

Jeri saw a stocky, gray-haired woman appear on the porch, beaming brightly as she waved a greeting. She had a squarish, no-nonsense face that lit with genuine pleasure at their arrival. Within minutes, Margaret Feeney—Mags to her friends—had firmly ensconced Jeri in a deliciously scented kitchen, setting out a glass of icy, spiced tea and a plate of freshly baked cookies with the flourish of a born hostess.

Wade remained outside to unload and stack the firewood. Mags carried on a delightful, nonstop stream of chatter as her shrewd eyes studied Jeri. Most of the conversation centered on Wade Evans, who was obviously a favorite conversational topic.

"The good Lord has a special place waiting for men like him," Mags said. "Davey and me—Davey's my grandson—well, we just would've frozen our fannies last winter if it weren't for Wade. He keeps my woodshed stacked to the rafters and won't take a penny for it."

Bustling constantly, Mags was slicing huge, red tomatoes for the line of sandwiches she was preparing. She stopped, wiped her hands on the skirt of her bibbed apron and grinned brightly at Jeri. "'Course, I've never known Wade to turn down a payment from my pantry," she said with a sly wink. "Jerome, neither. Gracious, those two could put it away." Mags chuckled to herself and proceeded to nearly empty her refrigerator onto the kitchen counter. Mags was all flying hands and elbows as she piled assorted fillings onto waiting slices of homemade bread. "Wade says my zucchini-cauliflower pickles are like the kiss of a wild woman...sweet as honey on the tongue but with enough bite to promise a night of wicked pleasure.''

Blinking in astonishment, Jeri stared at Mags. "Are we discussing the same man?'' she asked. Her tone clearly indicated skepticism. Somehow, Jeri couldn't quite believe her reluctant, tight-lipped partner capable of poetic cajolery. That sort of thing was more appropriately attributed to Jerome O'Brian and his silver-tongued Irish blarney.

Before Mags could answer, a small, dark-haired boy burst through the back door into the kitchen as though the devil himself was hot on his trail. His huge brown eyes shone with excitement as he panted noisily, trying to catch his breath.

"Gram!'' he finally gulped out. "Guess what? Wade said he'll take me back to the West Fork next week if it's okay with you. Is it, Gram?''

"Mercy, boy. Don't you two ever get enough fishing?''

Grinning, Davey shook his shaggy head. "Wade's teaching me to fly-cast, Gram. I've got to practice.'' Davey's freckled face shone with anticipation.

Mags smiled indulgently. "You clean 'em, hear? I've still got scales under my fingernails from last week.'' Mags's voice was stern, but her pale blue eyes sparkled with obvious love.

"I will, I promise. Thanks, Gram.''

Davey plowed through the back door, shoving it open at full speed, then letting it shut with a loud slam. Jeri could hear Murphy's excited yelps as Davey hollered Wade's name, his voice fading in the distance as he ran. She found herself laughing at the boy's exuberance, and marveling again at the complex, unknown facets of the enigmatic Mr. Evans.

Mags sat at the table and regarded Jeri thoughtfully. "I heard you were here, and I'm glad to finally meet you. I loved your father. The whole valley did. A fine man.'' Mags sipped her tea. "How are you and Wade getting on?''

Jeri was startled by the question. "We're adjusting. He didn't expect me to suddenly appear on his doorstep, and I'd assumed he'd be traveling the back country playing Daniel Boone and working his claims."

Mags blinked. "What on earth gave you a fool notion like that?"

Jeri gave a quick, nervous laugh. "When I saw my father last winter, he gave me the impression they spent most of the year trekking the wilderness like a couple of ancient fur trappers, living off the land and sluicing virgin, high-country streams." She gave a contrite grin. "I pictured two grizzled old prospectors, mules and all."

Mags responded with a delighted whoop of laughter. "Well, Jerome *did* love the mountains and took off for a few days or a week whenever he could. He was the wanderer, though, not Wade." Still smiling, Mags fixed Jeri with a penetrating stare. "Gold Creek was always Jerome's home, and it's still Wade's."

Jeri didn't miss the underlying significance of Mags's statement, and mumbled, "Of course, it is."

"Your company must be doing some good," Mags added. "It's been a long time since I've seen Wade smiling and acting like himself. He's been a hermit since..." Mags's voice trailed into silence.

"Since Daddy died?" Jeri asked softly.

"Yes. Since your daddy died." Mags stood and continued lunch preparations. The woman's back was to Jeri, but Mags seemed to anticipate Jeri's question.

"Yes, child," she said. "Wade grieves as much as you for that incorrigible, crusty old Irishman. In fact, I was right worried about him. After Jerome died, he holed himself up at the creek. No one saw hide nor hair of him for near on to a month."

The news should have stunned Jeri, but somehow it didn't. She knew instinctively how much Wade loved Jerome O'Brian. That love was the reason Wade was tolerating her presence, her invasion.

Meanwhile, Mags was neatly slicing the finished sandwiches, keeping a steady rhythm of chatter going, and Jeri pulled her thoughts back to the woman's conversation.

"...felt that Wade blamed himself for some reason. Lord only knows why. Doc Phelps said Jerome's heart was bad for years." Mags paused, lips pursed. She turned to Jeri. "You knew that?" she asked.

"No," Jeri said, surprised. "My father had a heart condition?"

"Yes, but Doc and I were the only ones that knew. He didn't even want Wade to know about it."

"Then why would Wade feel responsible? That doesn't make sense."

Lunch was ready. Mags refilled Jeri's iced-tea glass and sat down again. "I've never figured that out," Mags said. "But then, there's a lot about Wade Evans I never figured out."

"Like what?"

"Like how in the devil he manages to put food on his own table when he won't take his due."

"I don't understand," Jeri said, becoming increasingly puzzled.

"Rent. He won't take a penny unless you beg him. Always some reason. When Davey was sick, he told me to buy medicine with it. Twice last winter he took it, then used it to fill up my propane tanks."

"I didn't realize Wade had financial problems."

"Well, I wouldn't know about that," Mags said. "He seems to have enough to get by and enough to share. Just don't know how he manages, that's all."

Jeri mentally chewed that bit of information for a moment. "So, Wade owns this house?"

"This and half a dozen in the valley I know of. Same thing with all of us. The Blackthorns, for instance. Nice family. They live down by the Scott River junction. Know where that is?''

"Sort of.''

"They've got five kids. Every time the mill lays off, they live free. Then there's the Widow MacFarlen—Widow Mac, we call her—well, she—''

The back door flew open, interrupting Mags's testimonial. Davey skidded to the table, followed by Murphy, who looked at Margaret Feeney with anticipation. The dog ran a wet tongue anxiously across his whiskers and uttered a hopeful yip.

"We're starved, Gram," announced Davey.

Raising an eyebrow, Mags rose and picked up the plate of prepared sandwiches. "So I see. Now you go wash up, hear? You're not touching one of my fine sandwiches with hands like that.''

"Aw, Gram." Davey slunk from the kitchen just as the back door opened and Wade entered. Margaret Feeney lit up instantly.

"Done," he said, eyes roaming hungrily toward the luncheon platter. With a flashing grin he walked across the large kitchen in two strides and planted a kiss on Mags's wispy gray head. "I'll just wash up," he said cheerfully, and disappeared through the doorway.

Jeri had watched Wade's display of affection toward Mags with surprise and a strange sense of longing. She was gazing toward the doorway through which Wade had disappeared when Mags's voice filtered through her thoughts.

"I'm sorry," Jeri said. "I didn't hear you.''

Mags chuckled, opallike eyes shining perceptively, like penetrating beacons from her softly lined faced. "I was just saying how interesting it is that when Jerome knew his time on earth was ending, he managed to pull the two people he loved most in the world together.''

Jeri stared numbly. "Last winter . . . he knew?''

"That he did." Mags's smile broadened. "Makes you wonder what he had in mind, doesn't it?" Mags's expression left little doubt as to her own theory on the matter.

"Are you implying that my father was playing matchmaker, that he was trying to...to get Wade and I together?"

"I'm not implying anything, child," Mags replied, her eyes twinkling. "Just seems a coincidence, that's all."

Chapter Six

"Where's Jeri?"

"Out back with Davey." Mags busied herself in a sink full of soapsuds.

"Oh." Wade shuffled awkwardly. "We've got to go. Ben's expecting us to pick up her car."

"She'll be right back. Davey's showing her the tree house you and Jerome built for him." Mags rinsed a shimmering clear glass and angled a sly look at Wade. "Fine woman. You could do worse."

Wade reddened. "She's nothing to me but my partner's daughter."

"Nonsense," Mags replied cheerfully.

"You're poking your nose into something that's none of your business. Again."

Mags ignored Wade's scowling expression. "You can't live the rest of your life like a hermit just because you got your fingers burned once or twice. Life goes on, you know."

Frustrated, Wade stomped to the back door and threw it open. "Jeri! Get a move on!"

Mags continued to chatter, an annoying smile still plastered on her face. "You know she can't hear you. The tree house is down by the river."

"We've got to go," Wade grumbled, but sat docilely at the table as Mags set a fresh glass of iced tea in front of him.

"You going to help her with the store?"

Wade frowned. "What store?"

"The art store she's wanting to set up. You know, a place where she can sell paint and paper and other artsy stuff. I always wanted to paint myself, and Jeri's going to give me lessons." At Wade's incredulous stare, Mags nodded in satisfaction.

"An art store?" Wade raked his hair. "She never told me anything about it." He felt strangely resentful that Mags knew something about Jeri that he didn't.

"Hmphhh. And just when did you give her any indication that you would be interested in her plans?"

That hit a nerve. He'd been so certain she would run off as soon as she discovered that Gold Creek wouldn't make her a millionaire. "I just figured she'd be leaving soon."

"Is that what she told you?"

"No." She'd told him just the opposite, of course. Not that he'd believed her. "But anyone can see she doesn't belong here." Wade flinched under the sting of Mags's stern expression. "She's a city girl," he finished lamely. "Like her mama."

"Her mama," Mags repeated slowly. "And her mama was a fast woman with a taste for money, just like your ex-wife."

Wade carefully wiped the condensation off his glass, but didn't answer.

"Like mama, like daughter, right, Wade? Which means, of course, like father, like son...so why aren't you in jail like your daddy?"

Wade's voice was tight and angry. "Leave it alone, Mags."

"Or maybe you think she's like Denise, pulling the wool over your eyes so she can steal your land out from under you."

"Mags..." Wade's eyes were like granite.

"All right, I'll hush." Mags stood and smoothed her apron. "If you want to spend the rest of your life cringing in that cabin because you got your feelings hurt, that's your business." With that, she left the room, and Wade was alone with his thoughts and his memories.

Denise. She had been the most beautiful woman he'd ever seen. Red hair. It was natural, too, and she'd had the fire to go with it. The first time Wade had seen her, she'd been standing by the road, waving him to stop. A flat tire, she'd said. It was flat, all right, and he'd found out later that she'd turned away two offers of help, just waiting for Wade to come along. Waiting, like a spider in a web.

She'd gotten her painted claws into him so fast and so deep that Wade hadn't even known his own name. The next morning, he'd packed up his clothes, told Jerome goodbye and moved in with her.

What a fool he'd been. If Wade hadn't surprised her at her office that day, hadn't seen the blueprints spread across her desk and the dark man nuzzling her neck, Gold Creek meadow would be the center of a 240-unit retirement village right now. At first, Denise had tried to lie, but when she'd realized the game was up, she'd just shrugged and laughed. The dark man's eyes had sparkled in amusement until Wade made sure he had nothing to laugh about.

Wade had vowed never to make a fool of himself over any woman again. Not ever.

Wade headed the truck back up the highway toward Humbug and Ben Hawkins's Gas Station. The day was warm, almost too warm for comfort, and Jeri was glad both windows in the cab of the truck were open to allow the hot air complete access to her sticky body. The big Labrador

Incredible, isn't it? Deal yourself in right now and get 6 fabulous gifts ABSOLUTELY FREE.

1. 4 BRAND NEW SILHOUETTE ROMANCE™ NOVELS—FREE!

Sit back and enjoy the excitement, romance and thrills of four fantastic novels. You'll receive them as part of this winning streak!

2. A LOVELY BRACELET WATCH—FREE!

You'll love your elegant bracelet watch—this classic LCD quartz watch is a perfect expression of your style and good taste—and it's yours free as an added thanks for giving our Reader Service a try!

3. AN EXCITING MYSTERY BONUS—FREE!

And still your luck holds! You'll also receive a special mystery bonus. You'll be thrilled with this surprise gift. It will be the source of many compliments as well as a useful and attractive addition to your home.

PLUS

THERE'S MORE. THE DECK IS STACKED IN YOUR FAVOR. HERE ARE THREE MORE WINNING POINTS. YOU'LL ALSO RECEIVE:

4. FREE HOME DELIVERY

Imagine how you'll enjoy having the chance to preview the romantic adventures of our Silhouette heroines in the convenience of your own home! Here's how it works. Every month we'll deliver 6 new Silhouette Romance novels right to your door. There's no obligation to buy, and if you decide to keep them, they'll be yours for only $2.25* each! And there's no charge for postage and handling—there are no hidden extras!

5. A MONTHLY NEWSLETTER—FREE!

It's our special "Silhouette" Newsletter—our members' privileged look at upcoming books and profiles of our most popular authors.

6. MORE GIFTS FROM TIME TO TIME—FREE!

It's easy to see why you have the winning hand. In addition to all the other special deals available only to our home subscribers, when you join the Silhouette Reader Service, you can look forward to additional free gifts throughout the year.

SO DEAL YOURSELF IN—YOU CAN'T HELP BUT WIN!

*In the future, prices and terms may change, but you always have the opportunity to cancel your subscription. Sales taxes applicable in N.Y. and Iowa.

You'll Fall In Love With This Sweetheart Deal From Silhouette!

SILHOUETTE READER SERVICE™
FREE OFFER CARD

PLACE YOUR WINNING CARD HERE!

4 FREE BOOKS • FREE BRACELET WATCH • FREE MYSTERY BONUS • FREE HOME DELIVERY • INSIDER'S NEWSLETTER • MORE SURPRISE GIFTS

YES! Deal me in. Please send me four free Silhouette Romance novels, the bracelet watch and my free mystery bonus as explained on the opposite page. If I'm not fully satisfied I can cancel at any time, but if I choose to continue in the Reader Service I'll receive 6 Silhouette Romance novels each month for only $2.25 with no additional charge for postage and handling.

215 CIS HAYB
(U-S-R-09/89)

First Name _____ Last Name _____

PLEASE PRINT

Address _____ Apt. _____

City _____ State _____ Zip Code _____

Offer limited to one per household and not valid to current Silhouette Romance subscribers. All orders subject to approval.

SILHOUETTE NO RISK GUARANTEE
- There is no obligation to buy—the free books and gifts remain yours to keep.
- You'll receive books before they're available in stores.
- You may end your subscription at any time—by sending us a note or a shipping statement marked "cancel" or by returning any unopened shipment to us by parcel post at our expense.

PRINTED IN U.S.A.

Remember! To win this hand, all you have to do is place your sticker inside and **DETACH AND MAIL THE CARD BE-LOW.** You'll get four free books, a free bracelet watch and a mystery bonus. **BUT DON'T DELAY!**
MAIL US YOUR LUCKY CARD TODAY!

If card is missing write to:
Silhouette Reader Service, 901 Fuhrmann Blvd., P.O. Box 1867, Buffalo, N.Y. 14269-1867

rode, as usual, with his head out the window, ears and tongue both flopping in the breeze.

Jeri broke the silence. "I like Mags. She seems like a good person."

"The best."

"She sure thinks the world of you."

Wade gave an irritable grunt. "Can't believe everything you hear," he said, shifting uncomfortably. "What's all this about an art store?"

"Umm. I guess you're not the only person Mags talks about."

"Well?"

Jeri plucked at a piece of fuzz on her jeans. "It's just an idea I've been toying with. Mags seemed to think the valley's ready for a bit of culture." Wade laughed, and Jeri quelled him with a look. "Mags also said that there's a lot of talented people around here. She told me about a man in Scotts Valley who does exquisite wood carving and a lady down the road who weaves unusual wall hangings."

"What's that got to do with anything?"

"The store would offer them a place to display and sell their art." She was getting excited just thinking about it. "On consignment, you know? Plus there are lots of people who'd love to learn how to paint and draw, just for the enjoyment of it."

"Just where did you plan to put this...store?" A narrowed stare. "Be real careful with your answer, or we're going to get into one hell of a fight."

"That sounds like another one of your famous threats, and frankly, I'm getting sick and tired of— Oh, Wade, look."

Jeri leaned across Murphy, fighting him for a view out the cab window. They were slowing for a one-lane bridge ahead, and Jeri had spotted a peculiar object in the river. Bright yellow floats supported an engine and a long chute of some kind through which water and rock were rushing. Jeri recognized the men tending the metal beast.

"That's Nathan Loomis and his friends," she said. "They told me you could see their claim from the road. Can we stop for a minute?"

Wade's jaw had tightened. "No time," he muttered, and steered the truck onto the narrow span of wood and steel.

"That's a dredge, isn't it? It wouldn't take long, Wade."

"Later."

Jeri doubted it. Wade's face was taut, the muscles of his arms stiff as he grasped the steering wheel in a death grip. He was obviously upset about seeing Loomis's group, but Jeri couldn't understand why. At Happy Jack's, none of the miners had seemed to recognize Wade, and Wade hadn't appeared to have previously known any of them. It was strange, this odd behavior. Almost like fear.

She was still lost in thought when they reached Ben's. There, in all its battered, faded-yellow glory, was her trusty car. Well, maybe not so trusty after all, Jeri thought. But she'd seen a lot of miles with that dented little heap, and she had a certain affection for it. Besides, it would be great to have her own wheels again.

"Hey, Wade." A rangy man with slightly bowed legs appeared from the garage and walked toward the truck. "How's it going?" he asked, receiving Wade's curt nod before turning toward Jeri, who was fighting Murphy for the door handle. She won the battle and got the door open, but the dog hit the ground running, circling toward the back of the building like he knew exactly what he would find there.

The man gave a slightly buck-toothed grin and watched Jeri with curiosity, his pleasant gray eyes appraising her silently.

"You Miss O'Brian?"

"Yes. Ben, I presume?" Jeri asked, clued by the name neatly embroidered on his blue coveralls.

"Yes, ma'am," said Ben. "Pleased to meet you." He waved a greasy hand toward her car. "All set."

"I really appreciate this."

"No problem. I'll get your keys." Ben turned toward the small office. Wade stood by the doorway, looking grim. "Hey, man," Ben said cheerfully. "What the devil happened to you last night? I had the chessboard all set up."

Wade mumbled a response, and they went into the office. Jeri glared at his retreating back. Chess. He'd been coming over here to play chess with Ben Hawkins.

Might crimp my style a bit. What makes you think there are tables where I'm going? he'd told her.

Then he takes her to that dingy hellhole of a bar, pretending he's one of the regulars, and all the time he'd really intended to play chess.

Well, the joke was on her, all right. Wade must have had himself one heck of a good laugh watching her make a complete fool of herself.

Murphy trotted happily back into view. Beside him was a smaller dog, kind of a liver-colored pointer mix. The two animals came directly to Jeri and sat politely at her feet. Obviously, this was a formal introduction, dog-style.

"My, my," Jeri said. "And who is this ravishing creature?"

Murphy seemed to grin. The pointer looked rather shy, head bowed as she peeked up at Jeri with huge, liquid brown eyes.

"This is Lulu," Ben said, emerging from the office doorway. "She's a good dog. Swims. I never knew a dog to love water like Lulu."

Lulu looked up at the sound of her master's voice. All pretense of feminine coyness disappeared as she stood, quivering for the anticipated pat. Ben did not disappoint her, leaning to stroke her velvety head while Lulu's tail beat the air in frantic ecstasy. Murphy watched the procedure with a look of bored tolerance, perking up only when Lulu indicated a willingness to return to their romp. The animals darted out of sight once more, and Ben dropped a set of car keys into Jeri's hand.

"Thank you," she said. "What do I owe you?"

"It's taken care of," replied Ben.

Jeri blinked at him. "What do you mean, 'taken care of'?"

Ben shifted under her intense stare. "Well, I mean it's been paid already."

Stiffening, she straightened herself to full height and tossed her head back to stare straight into Ben's confused face.

"There has been a mistake. The bill couldn't have been paid, because *I* haven't paid it, and I always pay my own debts. Now, what do I owe you?"

"Well . . . er . . . it came to $683.27. But—"

"Will you take a check?"

Ben gulped and glanced nervously back toward the building. Wade was standing in the doorway watching, his lean body casually propped against the frame. His face was impassive, giving poor Ben no hint of assistance in handling his dilemma.

"Sure," Ben said finally, puzzlement and defeat tingeing his tone. "A check will be fine."

The river below widened into a calm, lazy meander, its warm green waters sparkling under the afternoon sun. Jeri had pulled her car onto the dirt shoulder south of the bridge and now sat watching the dredging miners. Her carefully packaged paintings lay in the back seat, and she wanted to get to the Klamath post office before it closed.

But her curiosity had gotten the better of her. Wade had other errands, so there was no one to keep her from trotting right down there and finding out what this mining business was all about.

With the stubborn determination of paternal parentage, she got out of the car and began the long descent toward the river. There was a path of sorts, and the slope wasn't particularly steep or treacherous. She reached level ground and was picking her way over the rock-strewed riverbank when Buck Mankin spotted her.

"Yo, Jeri," he called, waving. Jeri returned his greeting, then waved at Tad, who sat on his haunches holding what appeared to be a large green wok. The young man put the pan down and stood, grinning bashfully.

"Hi, Buck. Tad. I saw you from the road. You said it was okay to stop by—"

"Great!" Buck interrupted. "It's good to see you. Nat's down under." Mankin waved toward the river where the big dredge was roaring and pouring. "Can I get you something? Beer, soda?"

"No, thanks," Jeri said, laughing. "Just show me that darn dredge. I've been dying of curiosity."

Tad was watching her like a puppy watches its mama. He blushed as Jeri caught his look, and she grinned at him.

"What are you doing there?" Jeri pointed to the oddly shaped green object. The pan's flat bottom was covered with about an inch of black sand and gravel, and Tad deftly lifted it with one hand, thrusting it toward Jeri. She took it, surprised by its unexpected weight, and steadied it using both hands.

"What's this?" she asked.

"Concentrates."

Jeri gave him a blank look. "Concentrates of what?"

"That's the heavy stuff that settles out in the sluice," Mankin explained. "We run her for a couple of hours, then clean her out and pan the concentrates. That's where the gold is."

"If there is any," Tad added, then blushed furiously at his boldness.

Jeri handed the pan to Tad. "Go on, please. May I watch?"

"S-Sure," he stammered, then quickly went to work. Holding the pan with one hand, he scooped a small amount of water, then shook the pan in a circular motion, occasionally using the palm of his free hand to sharply swat the rim.

Jeri watched in amazement as light-colored sand and pebbles seemed to pop up to the surface of the thick, black sands. Tad thrust the pan just under the surface of the water, rotating it until the lighter material floated over the edge. He repeated the process until only about a cup of sand remained, all of it black and heavy.

Mankin had been busying himself with some hose fittings, but now stopped, coming to watch the final unveiling. Anticipation was heavy in the air. Scooping a small amount of clear water into the pan, Tad tipped it slightly and tapped until all the sand gathered heavily on one side. Then he began a gentle sideways sloshing motion that lifted one layer of sand from the pile and deposited it on the lower edge of the pan, where it was carefully washed into a large coffee can.

"We can process that later. Sometimes you find gold you can't even see," Mankin told her.

"How? If you can't see it, how can you get it out?"

Mankin shrugged. "There's ways. Mercury. Chemical leaching." He grinned at her. "Big hunks or tiny specks, gold is gold."

Tad's whoop interrupted Jeri's delighted laugh, and three faces peered into the green pan. As Tad continued to slosh the sand, bright yellow specks were being uncovered. Then some larger pieces.

"Those are tweezer pieces," Tad said, smiling proudly. Mankin whipped out a small vial already filled with water and about one-eighth inch of gold. He dried his index finger quickly on his shirt, then poked into the pan. When he held up his finger, Jeri could see the small gold flecks sticking to his skin. With a deft movement he touched his finger to the wet rim of the water-filled bottle and the gold dropped quickly to the bottom.

Tad and Buck repeated the process until all visible gold was in the tiny bottle and the heaviest concentrates had been poured into the coffee can.

"Not great," Buck said, "but we still have the rest to pan out." He pointed to a flat plastic tub containing at least half a bucket full of unprocessed sand and gravel.

Just then, a black-hooded figure broke the surface of the water. Loomis looked toward the shore, saw Jeri and waved happily. He wore a black rubber wet suit, complete with mask and air hose attached to his back harness. Reaching toward the dredge, he flipped something, and the metal monster coughed into silence. Loomis unbelted the harness, allowing it to float on the surface as he waded toward shore.

"Jeri. Good to see you," Nat said as he pulled off his mask and tossed it on a nearby towel. "Ready for your first lesson?"

She shook her head. "I wish I could," she said wistfully, "but I've still got some errands this afternoon. Maybe another time?"

"Anytime at all, girl. We'll be right here."

Something caught Loomis's attention, and he looked past Jeri, squinting into the low afternoon sun. Jeri heard the familiar panting sound and knew without turning what had caught Nat's eye. Murphy bounded happily up, blinking once at Loomis before turning his attention to Jeri. He leaped up and gave her one of his now-famous paws-on-shoulders, ear-to-ear juicy licks.

Jeri sputtered, then felt a huge shadow block out the sun and knew Wade was standing behind her.

"Howdy," Nathan said pleasantly. "Remember you from Happy Jack's. We never did meet proper. Name's Loomis."

He extended his hand, then withdrew it quickly to remove the massive orange vinyl gloves.

"This is Wade Evans," Jeri said primly. "My...partner." Although she didn't turn around, Jeri could practically feel the scowl at her choice of words.

"Pleasure." Wade's greeting was abrupt.

Oddly, Nathan seemed to take a liking to Wade, introducing him to Buck and Tad, then settling in to talk prospecting. Sighing, Jeri found a flat rock and sat down. Noting his friend's dejection, Murphy stretched in front of her, moaning in contentment, and laid his furry head on her feet.

Halfheartedly, Jeri listened to bits and pieces of the conversation, but most of it was so technical she didn't understand a word.

"It's a four-incher," Buck was saying. "Angled suction nozzle, Hungarian riffle system. Great recovery."

"What'll she pull?" Wade asked.

"Three hundred g.p.m.," Buck answered. "Eight horses in that engine." Wade nodded. "Want to try her?"

"Some other time," Wade said. "Looks like a nice unit, though." He turned toward Jeri. "Thought you wanted to mail your package."

She looked up at him. Way up. Standing over her, he seemed as tall as a redwood. There was a look in his eyes, a sweet-sad kind of expression that tugged at her, making her throat tight. He was a puzzle. A mysterious paradox of a man, invincible yet vulnerable, powerful as an oak and gentle as a butterfly's wings.

He was incredibly handsome.

With a sigh, Jeri slid her feet out from under Murphy's chin and stood. She smiled at Nathan.

"I guess I'd better be on my way," she said. "Thanks for the lesson."

"Come on back tomorrow and I'll take you under," Loomis said.

Jeri lit up. "I'd really like that." The thunderous expression on Wade's face froze her smile. "Of course, that pretty much depends on what's going on," she added.

"Well, anytime," Buck said.

Nodding tightly Jeri turned and headed back toward the path, stumbling over the rocky obstacles as she walked, completely lost in thought.

"Just what do you think you're doing?" Wade growled as he scooped up her elbow. "Those men could be ax murderers for all you know."

"That's ridiculous. I met them at Happy Jack's, and they're perfectly nice people." She lifted her chin and jerked her arm out of Wade's grasp. "Besides, they're going to teach me to dredge."

Wade's teeth clamped together. "No, they're not.'

"I beg your pardon?"

"No dredging."

"Excuse me, but you seem to have some kind of role mix-up here. I am not a child, and you are definitely *not* my father. I'll make my own decisions as I've been doing for the past eight years."

"Dredging's dangerous. I don't want to hear any more about it."

"You don't want to hear any more about it?" Her voice raised to a stunned squeak. "I will do whatever I want, with whomever I choose." Jeri planted her feet and jerked to a stop. "And if I want to dredge or skydive or swing on a trapeze, I don't need your permission to do so."

Wade whirled to face her. "It killed Jerome, and I'm not about to let it kill you, too."

Jeri froze. An expression of horror spread over Wade's face, as though he couldn't believe what he'd just said. His hand dropped from her arm as though burned, then he spun on his heels and walked away.

The small wooden sign was nearly obscured by thick vegetation; green vines and plants, twisting to escape the lush undergrowth of the forest beyond, wound up the post and drooped irreverently across its message: Humbug Creek Cemetery.

Pulling the car onto a flat dirt clearing across the road, Jeri stared at the sign, her fingers unconsciously tightening on the steering wheel like talons on prey.

She got out of the car and crossed the road, pausing briefly to run her fingertips lightly across the weathered wooden sign. The narrow pebbled path ribboned into the dense thicket of brush and trees, and Jeri followed it to a small bridge. The wood plank structure spanned a shallow trickle, beyond which lay a rusted, wrought-iron gate.

Layers of crisp leaves and dry pine needles crackled beneath her step, each foot sinking deeply into the decomposing foliage of past decades, unraked and undisturbed. Light filtered in random patterns through the thick canopy of birch, oak and pine that sheltered this place from the harsh elements of nature and man.

A heavy silence surrounded the cemetery, as though its quiet beauty was encased in a force field, an invisible dome capturing forever the aura of another time.

The air itself was thick, almost a living thing. It surrounded Jeri, enveloped her with affection, stroking and soothing like a lover's caress. She was overwhelmed by a deep sense of peace, contentment. Of being loved.

Left completely in its natural state, the cemetery at first glance appeared no different than the rest of the forest area. Pine cones bounced on the thick leaf-and-needle-quilted ground, and the area was overgrown with brush and vines. Only by carefully searching did one come upon small monuments constructed of assorted materials, some dating back as far as the 1850s.

Yet it was not sad but beautiful in its poignant simplicity. Jeri was calmed, reassured to know Jerome O'Brian was here, sharing nature's embrace with souls from a century to which he most certainly belonged.

A small, raked area caught Jeri's eye, and as she walked toward it, she saw fresh flowers cupped beside a small bronze marker. Instinctively she was drawn to it and reached down to trace the embossed welt of smoothly polished letters:

Jerome Patrick O'Brian
A Good Friend A Good Man

Jeri reached out to touch the freshly swept earth, flicking away an errant pine cone, smoothing the soft mound with her hand.

"Hello, Daddy," she said softly. "I've missed you."

It was late when Jeri returned to the cabin. She saw its windows, as dark as the surrounding night, and assumed Wade had already left for the evening. Feeling neither disappointment nor pleasure at his absence, she turned on the generator and lights, then sat at the kitchen table and lay the crumpled envelope in front of her.

She knew exactly what she would do now. It was all so clear and so simple. How sad that she had wasted so much time worrying about something so obvious. Her father's real legacy was his love of the land. The valley was the key, and Jeri would not leave. She knew she had two viable options. And the choice would be Wade's. Certainly, she had a preference, but she could live with either decision.

In any case, her problem would soon be resolved.

The front door of the cabin flew open with a vibrating blast, shocking Jeri into an instant state of panic. Leaping to her feet, she knocked the wooden chair over, and it fell to the floor with a cracking groan.

She stood, frozen, hand clutching at her throat as if to hold back a scream.

Wade loomed in the doorway, eyes blazing. "Where have you been?" His voice seemed to explode from his very core. Her eyes widened as his anxiety at her absence turned to fury. "Answer me," he snapped. "Where have you been?"

Jeri's mouth opened, but no sound came out, and she closed it, licking her lips before she tried again. "W-Why? What's...wrong?"

"What's wrong?" He stood before her, legs resolutely spread, clenched fists flexing as he held them rigidly at his side. "What the hell do you think is wrong? You disappear off the face of the earth for four solid hours...out God-knows-where in the dead of night—"

Abruptly, Wade stopped his verbal barrage, and Jeri saw through his anger, recognizing relief in his eyes.

"You were worried." She was stunned at the realization.

Wade seemed stunned at the realization as well, but he neither confirmed nor denied the fact. Throwing his arms up in a gesture of total frustration, he muttered a rather explicit description of what should be done with the entire situation, then turned and stomped out of the room.

It was several minutes before Jeri composed herself enough to follow him. She found him in the living room, sitting stiffly on the leather couch, his arms folded across his chest tightly enough to crack ribs and a furious black scowl on his face.

Somewhat shakily, Jeri managed to seat herself in the lounge chair across from him. Folding her hands together to calm their involuntary vibration, she cleared her throat to speak, silently begging her voice to be calm. "I'm sorry. I didn't realize...I didn't mean to worry anyone."

Wade continued to sulk darkly. "I couldn't care less what you do," he growled.

"Oh."

Wade shifted uncomfortably. "Maybe I was a little worried," he said finally, "but don't let it go to your head."

"That's not very likely," she said dryly. "You've never been one to boost my ego."

Muttering, he stood and paced the room with such blind intensity he nearly stepped on Murphy. The big Labrador eyed Wade's black mood with trepidation, wisely deciding to avoid his master's snit by moving to the farthest corner of the room.

Jeri sat mutely, watching Wade with increasing apprehension and growing confusion. What was wrong with this man, anyway? Earthquakes were more predictable.

This might not be the best moment to discuss options. On the other hand, it could possibly improve his foul humor. It certainly couldn't hurt. He was already mad enough to chew barbed wire.

"Wade, there's something we have to discuss."

"Umphh."

"This is good news."

"You're leaving?"

The cruel bite in his voice hurt, and Jeri winced as though she'd been slapped. "Actually, yes."

Wade's pacing stopped abruptly. He looked at her, a strange, sad kind of look that squeezed the air from her lungs. He started to say something, seemed to think better of it and simply nodded. Then he walked into the kitchen and sat, slumping as he rubbed his aching forehead.

Jeri followed, hesitating slightly, then seating herself across the table. She waited.

"When?" he finally asked.

"Well, that depends."

"On what?" Wade said skeptically.

"On options. And which one I take."

Wade scowled at her. "Honey, I don't have any idea what you're talking about, and I'm too dang tired to play games. If you've got something to say, then say it."

Jeri interrupted him by holding up her hand. "All right. Just listen."

Wade's jaw clamped shut, and he glared at her, motioning impatiently for her to continue. "I'm all ears."

She stared silently into her lap, squeezing her hands together into a single tight balled fist. She swallowed. Hard. When she spoke, her voice was softly threaded around a core of steel-hard determination.

"I want to buy you out, Wade. Name your price."

Chapter Seven

Several seconds of silence were finally ended by the sound of Wade's chair as it thunked back onto all four legs. Jeri looked up to see him leaning forward, staring incredulously. He gave a disbelieving snort, followed by a dry, humorless laugh.

"That's a good one," he said. "You had me going for a minute." Wade's tight smile compressed even further at Jeri's sober expression. "You're serious."

"Yes."

He shook his head slowly, a smile that could only be described as patiently indulgent playing on his lips. His expression was almost kind.

Not the response Jeri had anticipated. She'd expected anger. Or a flat, resounding no. Or even a go-to-hell. But not the kind of look a parent gives a wayward child.

Bristling silently, Jeri managed to maintain an impassive expression. "I want to pay what it's worth," she said, pleased with her reasonable tone.

"And just what do you figure that is?"

"Well, I hadn't exactly added it up, but I assume 165 acres of land is worth about a thousand an acre—"

"Two thousand," Wade interrupted. Jeri stared at him. "Inflation," he explained.

"Yes...all right then. Two thousand. And the cabin...uh..."

"Not too much," Wade speculated. "It's small, only two bedrooms." As usual, the table was cluttered with folders and loose papers. He rifled through them. "Let's see," he muttered, his somber expression not hiding the amused twinkle in his eyes. "Market value on the tax statement says forty-five thousand. It's probably worth more, but we'll use that."

"How kind," Jeri murmured, gritting her teeth.

His eyes narrowed. "Do you have any money?"

"I've managed to save a few dollars."

"How much?"

When she told him his lips twitched, then he grabbed a pencil and hunched over the table making an exaggerated show of performing the calculations. As he worked, he mumbled.

"Okay, half comes to about a hundred and eighty-three thousand." He saw her lips whiten and went in for the kill. "Bank will loan 80 percent, so you'll need—" his pencil scooted rapidly across the yellow tablet "—about four times more cash then you've got." He grinned brightly at her. "Then there's the mortgage, taxes and maintenance—"

"Stop right there." Jeri's face was white as a snowbank but her eyes shot copper darts. "You've made your point. You don't think I can hack it." She folded her arms tightly across her chest. "That will be *my* problem. You'll have your money. I know you could certainly use it."

A perplexed expression flickered across Wade's face, then disappeared. "How do you propose to get that much money?" he asked, his voice deceptively quiet.

"I repeat, that's my problem. As you said, I can get some of the money from a bank. That goes straight into your pocket."

"And the small matter of the down payment?"

"Well, if you'd be willing to take a second mort—" She stopped as his head rocked back and forth, and her jaw clamped in stubborn determination. "I'll get it."

Wade's expression hardened. "What you'll get is the whole kit-and-kaboodle repossessed in two months. No thanks, honey. I've no intention of giving Gold Creek up to the highest bidder."

"My paintings bring in money. And I'll get a job. Two, if I have to," Jeri said, a small note of desperation creeping into her voice.

"No."

"Wade—"

"Dammit, it's not for sale. Not now, not ever. Got it?"

Pushing himself away from the table, he stood, tossed the scattered papers untidily back into the folder and strode from the room.

Alone in the kitchen, Jeri took several deep breaths and tried to suppress her disappointment. She was not particularly surprised by Wade's refusal, but after what Mags had said about Wade's financial situation, Jeri had allowed herself a small glimmer of hope.

Well, what did she expect? Jerome O'Brian would've lived on dandelions and blackberries before he would sell a dream. So would Wade Evans. And Jeri couldn't really blame him, because she felt the same way. In the farthest recesses of her mind, she knew Gold Creek would always be safe. The knowledge gave surprising comfort.

On to option two. With a sigh, Jeri went into the living room. A newspaper, opened wide and held strategically, blocked Wade's expression. Jeri assumed it would be appropriately sour. She walked to the front window. It was black as pitch outside. No moonlight, no stars. Somber.

It matched her mood.

"You win," she whispered, as though a mere thought slipped out unbidden.

The newspaper rustled.

"I'll leave tomorrow." She spoke quietly, still looking out the window, not seeing the myriad of emotions flickering across Wade's face. He was silent for several minutes.

"Where'll you go?" he asked.

She shrugged. "I'll see if there's room at the lodge. If not, there are motels in Yreka. Then I'll start looking for something I can afford."

Wade was obviously skeptical. "I hope you don't expect indoor plumbing."

She silenced him with a cold, hard stare. "That, too, is my problem," she informed him frostily. Reaching for the doorknob, she pulled the front door open and, not bothering to close it behind her, stepped out into the cool night air. Wade appeared in the doorway behind her, casting a shadow across the porch.

"It'll cost an arm and a leg for lodges and motels," he said quietly.

Jeri shrugged.

Wade cleared his throat. "You'll use up half your downpayment money in a couple months."

"I'll get a job." Her voice was flat. "I'd have to anyway."

"Yeah, maybe."

He stepped out onto the porch and stood against the railing. He was ten feet away, but Jeri could feel his presence as though it were mere inches. The skin on her arms tingled. Her neck felt a little prickly.

Just the soft summer air, she told herself. Nothing more than the night and the crickets and the fragrance of the forest waking up her hormones.

Ignore it. Ignore him.

Jeri walked across the porch and settled herself on the top step, increasing their distance by a few precious feet.

"I don't suppose there's any big hurry," he said.

Jeri wrinkled her nose. "About what?"

She heard a shuffling noise, turned and saw his booted foot pushing an acorn across the rough wooden planks.

"You moving." He added quickly, "I mean, right away."

She stared at him. "What on earth are you talking about?"

"It won't hurt for you to stay here until you find a place." Wade wasn't looking at her. He was watching the acorn, then he was glancing out across the forest. But he wasn't looking anywhere close to where Jeri sat, staring at him in bewilderment.

"I thought you wanted me out?"

"I do," he snapped. "But...I mean, now that you're trying to find someplace, no sense my kicking you out and letting you go broke."

"I won't go broke." Her statement was punctuated with a haughty sniff.

Finally, Wade exploded. "Oh, for crying out loud! Go if you want, stay if you want. It's nothing to me."

The sturdy porch vibrated as Wade headed toward the cabin door with two major-league stomps. Jeri called his name, and he turned.

"Thank you," she said. "If it wouldn't put you out, I really appreciate the offer."

He nodded brusquely, then disappeared into the cabin, closing the door behind him.

Sweet darkness enveloped her as she mulled the surprising turn of events. Subconsciously, she'd known Wade would never sell. Moving out had been option two. Having Wade ask her to stay on while she looked for a place...well, that hadn't even been covered in option three.

Unconsciously she wrapped her arms around her shoulders, softly stroking her upper arms as she rocked slowly, smiling, mentally thanking the responsible deity. Then she stood, turning to reenter the cabin.

She froze, a scream caught in her throat.

Staring out of the blackness, almost level with her face, were two glowing, yellow, evil-looking eyes. Her scream finally broke loose, then another and another, renting the air like high-pitched death cries.

When Wade threw open the door, she was standing rigid with terror. To her profound shock, Wade's face broke into a wide grin. Murphy had bounded onto the porch a step behind Wade and now stood watching the beady yellow eyes, wagging his tail wildly.

"About time you showed," Wade said to the glowing beads. "Began to think you were coyote-ate."

The eyes fell from their five-foot height to porch level. Murphy bounded to greet them.

"Oh, my goodness," Jeri whispered, holding her hands tightly in front of her chest to stop their frantic trembling. "It's a raccoon."

"Well, if it's not, its mamma'll sure be surprised," Wade said cheerfully. "Come on...come here," he coaxed gently. "That's it."

The raccoon cautiously eyed Jeri as it hunkered slowly toward Wade. Murphy was happily sniffing the animal, and it ignored the rather personal nature of the dog's nosey perusal.

Wade lowered himself, sitting back on his heels, hand extended encouragingly, and the animal moved warily into petting distance.

"This is Rocky," Wade said, scratching the raccoon's soft underbelly as it flipped onto its back and began to wriggle in ecstasy.

"I rather assumed you were acquainted," Jeri mumbled. Rocky stopped squirming and stared, his shiny masked eyes observing Jeri with an odd combination of annoyance, curiosity and surprising intelligence.

"He started coming around about three years ago," Wade told her. "He was just a cub when he discovered a sweet tooth and kept coming back to feed it." Wade chuckled softly as the tiny handlike paws insistently tugged at his fingers.

"Looking for dessert?" he asked. Rocky cocked his head, the small button-black nose quivering on the tip of his pointed snout.

"What does he eat?"

"Most anything. He's partial to chocolate, but he'll have to settle for grapes tonight. That's all we've got."

Wade shook loose the grasping little fingers and stood. "Wait here," he instructed, and the raccoon seemed to give an acquiescent nod as Wade disappeared into the cabin to fetch his treat.

Jeri's heart had gradually resumed a normal rhythm, and she slowly knelt on the porch to get a better look at the fascinating creature. Rocky's snout twitched in her direction. He glared at her belligerently. Hesitantly Jeri extended her hand, hoping the raccoon would approach, but he only sniffed, watching her with obvious disdain.

"Try these."

Wade stood in the doorway holding out a handful of shiny green grapes, and Jeri took them with a hesitant smile. She tentatively offered one. Rocky stared at the grape, then up at Wade as though he were Benedict Arnold.

Betrayed or not, he was still being offered a grape, and the raccoon wanted it. He finally scootched close enough to reach out, dexterously plucking the prize from Jeri's palm.

She lit up with delight, and Wade watched, enjoying her childlike pleasure. When Jeri looked up at him, her eyes shone like molten gold, and the soft cabin light reflected the excited flush of her cheeks.

"He's absolutely adorable," she said, breathless, then laughed as Rocky cleverly manipulated the grape, agilely turning it for a thorough inspection before raising it to his mouth. He nipped it, almost delicately, using sharp needle-like teeth to shred the juicy pulp.

Murphy, not to be ignored, seated himself firmly next to the raccoon looking hopefully at Jeri.

"Not you, too?" she chided. Murphy looked sheepish, but uttered a low, optimistic whine.

Wade gave a husky laugh. "That dumb dog wants anything the raccoon gets. He's afraid he'll miss something."

With a shrug and a chuckle, Jeri presented Murphy with his very own grape. Gingerly positioning his teeth on the slick round surface, Murphy sucked it into his mouth then crunched it with relish. Rocky, meanwhile, impatiently inched forward and was offered another delicacy for his trouble.

"Doesn't he need water?" asked Jeri. "I read somewhere that raccoons have to wash their food."

"If there was water handy, he'd dunk it," Wade replied. "He's made a mess of Murphy's water bowl more than once. But he's sure not going to turn down a meal if he can't."

As though to prove the point, Rocky scooted forward until he was almost on Jeri's lap and grabbed her hand with nimble paws. The raccoon opened her fingers, rubbing his padded palm across hers to assure himself it was truly empty. The tiny paws were thin-fingered and knuckled exactly like miniature human hands, but had long, sharpened doglike claws. The smooth, velvety fur extending down his forearm covered the back of his paws, but the palms were incredibly soft-skinned and hairless.

Jeri laughed at the animal's quizzical expression as Rocky looked pleadingly up at Jeri, then down at her empty hand. From behind her back, Jeri produced the coveted fruit, dropping one into her open palm. Rocky snatched it greedily. Murphy anxiously reminded Jeri of his presence.

Jeri looked up and was surprised at Wade's soft, almost reverent expression. He was watching her intently as she played and laughed, and his eyes had deepened to a dusky teal. His full mouth seemed almost vulnerable now, stripped of its familiar, tight-lipped constraint.

Wade was mesmerized, totally captivated. To him, Jeri's laughter seemed to bounce through the night like the tinkling of a million silver bells.

She was so pretty when she smiled, he thought. Sweet. Innocent. Her laughter sent shivers skittering to the soles of his feet. It was like an angel's song, that laugh. A melody from heaven.

As Jeri watched the animals, face shining, eyes wide with delight, Wade realized that a man would kill for that look.

Or die for it.

What would it be like to have her look at him that way? A vision suddenly appeared in his mind's eye like a Technicolor movie. Jeri was laughing in the meadow, surrounded by tousle-haired children who looked a lot like him. Then she saw him and stretched her arms toward him. And her eyes were shining with love.

The image overwhelmed him. He saw himself walk into her arms, saw her lips part for his kiss and his mouth would come down on hers.

He could actually taste her sweetness.

"Wade!" Jeri's voice was puzzled and insistent. He started, staring at her in momentary confusion. She held out the grapes, and he looked at them stupidly. "Here, take them," she said, motioning.

"Why?" He felt like a fool, as though he'd just been plucked out of midair and zipped into someone else's skin.

"I want to get my sketchpad," she said. "Can you keep him here?"

"Who? Oh...sure." Wade took the grapes, bending down to hand one to an impatient raccoon as Jeri brushed by and disappeared into the cabin. With a heavy sigh, Wade looked into Rocky's glossy black eyes.

"I must be losing my mind," he mumbled. Rocky and Murphy both appeared to empathize with Wade's problem, offering solemn, if silent, condolence.

When Jeri returned, she positioned herself in the shadows so she could sketch without disturbing her sensitive subject. She worked quickly for several moments.

Wade cleared his throat nervously.

Distracted, she looked up questioningly. He made another unsettled noise before he spoke.

"I...uh, that is— Ow! Dang it, Rocky, watch your manners."

The animal, tired of waiting, had reached out, prying at Wade's hand with its sharp claws. Jeri's lips twitched in amusement. Wade scowled. Rocky didn't appear to be the least bit contrite.

"I told Davey I'd take him up to West Fork tomorrow," Wade said.

"That will be nice," Jeri replied. Her attention returned to the sketch pad.

"Fishing," Wade added.

Jeri looked up. "He seems like a sweet boy," she said, "and he certainly thinks the world of you."

"I've known him since he was no bigger than a toad's tail," Wade said flatly. "He was just a pup when his folks died and Mags took him in."

Charcoal sticks moving rapidly, Jeri shaded and contoured as the images took life under her hands. As she concentrated, she unconsciously chewed on her tongue, its rosy tip peeking out at the corner of her mouth.

Wade stared at it.

"Do you fish?" he asked.

"Umm? Oh, sure. My father took me with him all the time when I was little." She looked up and grinned. "I even baited my own hook."

Wade smiled. "I pity the worms." He pursed his lips, eyebrows lowered in concentration. "Want to go?"

Jeri's head snapped up, and she stared at him in surprise. "Go?"

"Fishing," he said, exasperated.

A smile of genuine pleasure lit her features. At that moment, Wade was sure she was the most beautiful woman God had ever put on the Earth.

"I'd love to go fishing with you," she said. "But I think Davey would be hurt and disappointed to share you."

"Maybe," he acknowledged.

"Will you invite me again?"

"Maybe."

Wade stood, showing his empty palms to the disheartened animals. "Gone," he announced, unnecessarily. Four shiny eyes stared at him pitifully.

Stretching, he glanced peripherally at Jeri. To his chagrin, she was staring right at him. He coughed.

"Guess I'll turn in," he said.

She nodded, smiling.

"Might as well come in yourself." Wade looked at Rocky. "He'll be leaving now that the food's gone," he said firmly, staring at the raccoon as though issuing an order rather than stating a fact.

To Wade's consternation, Rocky simply sat on his haunches and began a leisurely bath. Jeri chuckled softly, and Wade went into the cabin muttering to himself.

Setting her sketch pad down, Jeri watched the animal groom itself and mulled the surprising events of the evening. It was all too good to be true. Wade Evans was acting like...

Then she shook her head, dropping it forward as her shoulders slumped. No wonder he's mellowed out, she reminded herself sadly. She would be leaving soon. His problem has just been solved.

It had been two days since Jeri had made her decision to leave Gold Creek. Jeri had been listening to the insistent chug of the engine long before Wade's truck finally roared into the clearing. Busily removing the still-wet painting from her easel, she rushed to tuck it out of sight in her room. This was a very special painting, a gift for Wade, but Jeri wanted it to be perfect before she presented it, so she only worked on it when he wasn't around.

Jeri watched through the window as Murphy waited politely for Wade to get out of the truck before leaping from seat to dirt in a single bound.

"Darn dog never lets *me* get out first," she mumbled in consternation.

She saw Wade look toward the cabin briefly, then toward Jeri's battered car before walking around the truck to unhitch the tailgate. He lifted a fifty-pound bag of concrete as though it were a pound of sugar, throwing it on his shoulder and striding out of view around the side of the cabin.

Jeri loved to watch him when he wasn't aware of her. He was so strong, yet moved with surprising grace and agility. She loved the way his muscles corded, straining against the thin fabric of his shirt, flexing and surging with every movement.

Her stomach began to tighten and warm, the uncomfortable heat radiating through her torso. Stiffly, she turned away, knowing a bothersome, prickly sensation would soon begin to creep into areas of her body where she would prefer not to prickle.

Annoyed with herself and the world in general, she went to her room and changed into a swimsuit. She'd spent the past two mornings canvassing banks and harassing the valley's only realty office. The news was not good. Wade had been right about just how far her savings would stretch, but she had no intention of admitting it.

Now she felt restless. Since Wade had been so upset the other night when he couldn't find her, Jeri had dutifully stayed close to the cabin. Wade had taken to watching her like a hunting owl, and although it annoyed her, she was trying to avoid another argument. Now she needed to get away.

She thought of Nat Loomis and his friends. This was the day, she decided, to take them up on their invitation. She'd earned a bit of relaxation, and if Wade didn't like it, he could simply pound sand. Assuming, of course, that he found out. Jeri rather hoped to make her escape without a major scene.

Pulling on her jeans and tossing a ragged white T-shirt over her modest one-piece swimsuit, Jeri gathered up a couple of towels, pocketed her car keys and headed for the door.

She hit the porch at full stride, quietly closing the cabin door, then headed toward her car at a full gallop. Hopefully, she would be on her way before Wade came back into the clearing for the standard, where-the-devil-are-you-going interrogation.

She grasped the car door handle. Murphy appeared at her side, panting and excited. She patted his tawny head.

"Shhhhh . . ." she whispered.

Murphy understood the significance of the covert operation, and let Jeri know by replying with a resounding yelp. Jeri moaned.

"Hey! Where the devil are you going?" Wade bellowed, appearing behind her.

Blast it.

Pasting a casual, oh-there-you-are look on her face, she smiled and turned toward him.

"Hi," she said. "Nice morning."

He looked at the towels clutched tightly in her hand, then stared evenly at her.

"Going swimming?" he asked.

Nervously, she nodded. "Sort of."

He pursed his lips, eyebrows lowered thoughtfully. "You can swim at the creek," he pointed out.

"Yes, well...I thought I'd go down to the river." She saw Wade nod, his face blank, eyes ominous.

"By Walker Bridge, I'd bet." Wade's tone was unpleasant.

Jeri fumed. "And you'd win," she snapped, chin lifting defiantly, eyes darkening in anger. "They've offered to teach me how to dredge, and I'm going to take them up on it."

Wade's jaw clamped, and his cheek twitched. He seethed with fear and fury. She was going to defy him, going dredging with a bunch of strangers who would drop her like a cork in the current and go on about their business. Even in the shelter of the creek, dredging was dangerous, but the river was even worse. It was wide and deep and fast.

Wade had every intention of getting a grip on himself so he could rationally explain the danger. Then he noticed the pink swimsuit outlined beneath the thin cotton of her shirt. His stomach twisted into a jealous knot, and the words blurted out before he could stop them. "Just how do you plan to pay them for the lessons?"

He saw Jeri's face pale in shock, and he regretted his remark the moment it was out of his mouth. What in the world was wrong with him? Wade tried to apologize, to swallow his words, but it was too late.

"How dare you say that to me?" Jeri bristled like a stepped-on porcupine. "Listen, you overgrown, oversexed chauvinist, not every man in the world goes through life unzipping his jeans at the mere sight of a female form."

She yanked the car door open so hard that the tiny car seemed to shudder in pain.

"Jeri, wait—"

"And furthermore," she said, seething, "what I do and who I do it with is none of your blasted business." She shot him a look laced with pure poison. "Got that, buster?"

Flinging the towels onto the front seat, she turned to get into the car, only to have Wade grab the waistband of her jeans and yank her backward with enough force to jar her teeth. She whirled on him like a cornered cat, but he snagged both her wrists in one hand and, to her shock, reached into her pants pocket. Ignoring her outraged gasp, he deftly pulled out her car keys, held them in front of her nose then dropped them into his shirt pocket and released her hands.

"Stay here," he commanded, then turned and marched toward the cabin. Jeri watched in stunned silence, then flew into a murderous rage reminiscent of Jerome's famous Irish tantrums.

"You arrogant bully," she screamed at his retreating back. "You . . . you . . ." She vainly tried to conjure an insult vile enough. "Give me my keys! You've got no right . . . come back here!" Her entire body was rigid, vibrating with outrage and furious indignation. Wade had disappeared into the cabin, leaving Jeri wildly babbling to herself. Frantic for a victim, she turned on Murphy.

"This is all your fault," she hollered at the hapless animal. Murphy's eyes liquefied like melted fudge, ears dipping low, big yellow head drooping pathetically as he cringed at the verbal attack.

With a soft whine, Murphy slunk forward on his belly until his muzzle was an inch from Jeri's knees. Then his head dropped, and he gently licked her bare ankle.

"Oh, heavens," Jeri moaned, dropping to her knees and throwing her arms around the miserable beast. "I'm sorry. It's not your fault at all," she whispered, and was rewarded by the soft, swishing sound of a wagging tail.

A pair of denim-covered knees appeared in front of her, and her tattered tennies plopped into the soft dirt like two acorns dropping from a tall oak.

"If you're through caterwauling, we can get started."

Jeri looked up, blinking through the sun's glare at the figure towering above her. Quickly she stood. It was better to face an armpit than a knee.

"Started doing what?" she asked, then grunted as he slung a small backpack into her chest.

"Carry this," he said, then turned and walked rapidly toward the knoll bordering Gold Creek. Jeri saw he had a much larger pack strapped on his back. Confused, she stood rooted to the ground and stared at him.

"Better come on," Wade called, without looking back. "It takes a while to get there."

"Get where? Where are we going?"

Wade stopped, turning at the waist to look back at her. His hands were held high on his chest, thumbs tucked behind the straps of the backpack. Jeri noticed that his expression was tinged with sadness.

"I thought you wanted to dredge," he said.

Chapter Eight

They hiked for about thirty minutes, following the creek upstream into the tree-thickened heart of the forest. Jeri noted that Wade had been exceptionally silent, except for perfunctory, cautionary comments about snapping branches and slippery rocks. Wade allowed Murphy to take the point position, and the animal happily scouted the trail ahead, returning occasionally to sound a canine all-clear signal.

The creek took a sharp bend, its slowing waters fanning into a deep, boulder-bordered pool. Jeri saw that Murphy sat on the bank, waiting patiently. When they reached him, Wade stopped, dropping his pack to the ground. He stared solemnly at the quiet green water.

"Is this it?" Jeri asked. Wade gave an abrupt nod.

Scanning the surroundings, Jeri saw nothing out of the ordinary—rocks, trees, bushes and water. No dredge.

She nestled her pack in a cradle of tree roots and eyed Wade suspiciously. He seemed to read her thoughts.

"It's over there," he said, pointing to a large clump of brush.

Jeri followed him down the bank, helping as he pulled away large branches to reveal a khaki-colored tarp mounded beneath. With a deft flip, Wade tossed the tarp aside to reveal a neatly stacked pile of equipment—gasoline cans, shovels, crowbars, buckets. And one very large dredge.

"It doesn't look like it's been used in a while," Jeri said carefully, watching Wade's tight, sad expression.

"Not since last winter."

Proceed with caution, she told herself. She had a lot of questions about her father's death, and somewhere, buried in that clump of metal and plastic tubing, were the answers. Wade could unlock that secret, she was certain, but not if she spooked him.

She cleared her throat, forcing her voice to be light and cheerful. "Was Daddy with you?"

His jaw hardened. "Yes."

Turning away, he walked down the embankment. Jeri followed, deciding to broach the subject later. She was certain of one thing, however. They were not going to leave until she had some answers, and, if necessary, she would tie Wade to the nearest tree until she got them. Well, that might be a bit ambitious, she decided, since he outweighed her by about eighty pounds, but she would think of something.

She simply *had* to know the truth.

It took another half hour to pull the heavy machine from bank to stream and hook up the dizzying array of hoses and nozzles. Wade worked with practiced efficiency, patiently answering Jeri's questions.

When fully assembled, Jeri saw that the dredge was an odd-looking composite of parts floating on two bright yellow plastic pontoons.

"What's that for?" Jeri asked as Wade tossed a length of hose capped by a cagelike device.

"Sucks water into the pump. Pushes out through this hose—" Wade wiggled the subject length of plastic "—and creates the suction.'' Wade smiled as Jeri wiped her sweat-dampened forehead. ''Hard work, huh?''

Jeri nodded, her expression sour. This was certainly more effort than she'd realized. ''When can we start?''

''Now.''

Wade screwed an angled, wide-mouthed steel nozzle with a rubber-gripped handle on one end of the sixteen-foot length of hose.

Finally, Jeri watched as Wade gave the engine cord a pull. The engine sputtered, and he fiddled with a lever. Then he yanked the cord again, and the engine roared to life. Water began to gush into the sluice, rushing over the riffles then out the open end, back into the creek. Jeri decided that the contraption was like a noisy recirculator, sucking the water and gravel from the front and dumping it out the back.

''It's ready,'' Wade said loudly enough to be heard over the engine noise as he sloughed through the calf-deep water to the bank. He shucked his shirt and pants, revealing a pair of snug-fitting, form-flattering swim trunks. ''You shouldn't need a wetsuit,'' he said. ''The water's warm this time of year. Let me know if you get cold.''

Jeri stripped to her swimsuit and walked tentatively toward the water. ''What do I do?''

''Come here.''

She complied and found herself being trussed in a harness as complex as a skydiver's. A black tube hung limply over her shoulder. A mouthpiece was attached to the end of the tube, and Wade held it to her lips.

''Put this in your mouth and bite into this rubber part with your teeth. That's good.''

He reached up with his thumb and forefinger and pinched her nose closed. Her eyes widened in shock.

''Breathe in,'' he instructed.

She did, and a great rush of dry air dived down her throat, inflating her lungs until she thought they would burst. With a muffled gurgle, she pushed his hand away and yanked the mouthpiece out.

"You're trying to kill me," she gasped.

Wade grinned. "Unless you've got gills, you'll be needing this. Try again." She eyed him skeptically.

Strapping on his own harness he said, "Look. I'll show you." He proceeded to demonstrate. "Nothing to it. Only you've got to stop sucking air when your lungs are full. Okay?"

"Okay," she mumbled, unconvinced.

After a few more tries, she got the hang of it and was just thinking this whole dredging business was simple enough when Wade snapped a lead-studded belt around her waist and her knees nearly buckled. She gaped at him. Maybe he really *did* have murder on his mind.

"This'll keep you under," he said.

"I should say so," Jeri mumbled with obvious suspicion.

He laughed. "If you don't wear it, that sweet little rear of yours will keep popping to the surface like a marshmallow. Something to do with fat content."

"Then you'd better wrap one around your head," she snapped indignantly.

He chuckled and thrust a scuba mask at her. She snatched it from him, not particularly pacified.

"Spit in it," he said.

"What?"

"Spit in it. So it won't fog up."

He demonstrated on his own mask, then dipped it into the water and slipped it over his head. "See?"

"That is positively gross," Jeri said, giving her chin a haughty tilt. "I won't do it."

Wade shrugged. "Suit yourself. Ready?"

With a gulp, she nodded.

"Okay, now listen up. We'll be down about eight feet. It's fairly sheltered, but there's still a sizable current, so be ready for it."

Jeri nodded obediently.

"Don't be moving any rocks unless I say so. Get careless, and we'll be spending a lot more than one afternoon down there. Got it?"

Jeri snapped to attention and saluted sharply. "Got it, sir!"

Wade smiled. "I'm glad you finally learned some manners."

She gave him a withering look as he took her arm, leading her toward the center of the creek but carefully avoiding the deep-pooled area. When the swirling waters were nearly breast high on Jeri, he stopped.

"Take the regulator," he instructed, holding it to her mouth. "There. Now put on your mask." He waited until Jeri complied, adjusting the tight fit under her nose. She blinked at the fuzzy, water-spotted view. Wade laid his hand flatly between her shoulder blades, urging her forward. "Put your face underwater and breathe. Take it slow, now. Just get used to it."

Cautiously, she leaned forward until her face just broke the surface. If she hadn't had a mouthful of rubber, she would have gasped at the beauty of the underwater landscape. Without the distorted light refraction on the surface, the secret world of the creek was spread before her in clear, vivid color—a collage of green moss, multihued pebbles glimmering in the silt like shining jewels and bright cinnabar-colored patches adorning speckled granite boulders.

Without conscious thought, she bent forward for a closer look, and cold water rushed into her ears, filling her brain with a dull roar. She straightened instantly, wanting only to eliminate the unpleasant sensation.

"That wasn't so bad, now was it?" Wade asked, flicking a fat droplet from the end of her nose. "Try it again. Put your whole head under this time."

"I . . . uh . . . don't like the water in my ears."

"Okay with me," he replied, turning around as though to guide her back to the bank.

"Wait!" She was annoyed by the desperation in her voice. "I want to learn . . ."

"Well, if you're going down there," he said, pointing to the deepest part of the creek, "those cute little ears will just have to get a bit damp."

Jeri felt incredibly foolish. "Yes, of course. What do you want me to do?" His eyebrow arched. "All right," she said, thoroughly peeved, and shoved the hated regulator back in her mouth.

This time Jeri tried to ignore the unpleasant pressure of the water in her ears and soon was surprised to find the roar had become a distant, rather soothing rhythm. She even bent far enough to reach a shimmering white, egg-shaped rock, just touching it with her hand as her view began to distort. Clasping the smooth pebble in her hand, she blinked to clear her eyes, but within seconds she saw only a blurry cloud.

Wade will just love this, she thought with irritation. Straightening suddenly, she tried to turn away from him as soon as her head cleared the surface, but he grabbed her arm and turned her toward him, his face mirroring first concern, then amusement.

"How's the view?" he asked.

"Very funny," she snapped, yanking the mask off with her free hand.

"What's that?"

Jeri looked blankly down at her palm. "Oh. Isn't it pretty? So white and smooth. A perfect egg."

Wade took it, examining it closely. "Milk quartz," he pronounced. "Nice piece." He deftly tossed it toward the bank where it landed almost on top of Jeri's towel. Then he turned toward her, watching patiently. With a sigh of defeat, Jeri spit as delicately as possible into her mask, smearing it thoroughly, then rinsing as Wade had done. Nose wrinkled in disgust, she slipped it over her head and glared at him.

"Now, coach?" she asked, not bothering to hide her sarcasm.

"Now."

The brief lessons had not prepared Jeri for the sensation of dropping like a rock into the deep, clear pool. Water rushed her like a thousand angry linebackers, tackling her entire body in waves.

To her horror, panic began to bubble up in her stomach as the creek bed dropped beneath her and the comfort of the surface shot away from her grasping hand. She began to struggle, writhing desperately as the terror invaded her, but the weight belt did what it was intended to do, keeping her firmly on the bottom.

She wanted to scream, to cry out like a child, but all she could do was to gurgle weakly. Wade would laugh, she thought bitterly. *This is exactly what he wants me to do. Oh, Lord. He was right. I can't do this.*

Suddenly Wade's arm was around her, holding her against him in an underwater embrace. His hand stroked her cheek, her hair. Jeri's eyes were tightly closed. At his touch, she opened them, staring at the familiar hazel eyes watching her from behind the protective plastic mask wall. He nodded his head, giving her encouragement and support with his eyes, while his strong hand kneaded the tension from her lower back.

Soon, her breathing became slower, more normal, and her heart was beating rhythmically, if a bit fast. Through eye and hand signals, Wade asked if she wanted to surface. She shook her head.

Wade was with her. She could do anything.

He motioned for her to stay put, then pushed himself in a half swimming, half crawling motion across the rocks at the edge of the pit. When he returned, he was dragging the dredge nozzle and the massive hose to which it was attached. He braced himself against the rock wall and lowered the nozzle to the gravel-covered bottom. Jeri could see the swirling current as water was powerfully sucked into the jaws of the nozzle, pulling sand, silt and gravel along with the flow.

Wade signaled for her to come closer, then began to tug on her thigh. She looked at him in shock. This was definitely not the time or the place for that sort of thing.

With a sense of embarrassment, she realized that he wanted her to straddle the big hose, like riding a horse. It seemed silly, but she did it. He stood behind her, grasping her hands and lowering them to the handle of the nozzle. Holding his hands over hers, he showed her how to maneuver the beast, allowing it to take the proper mix of water and gravel to avoid clogging. When it reached a rock too large for its greedy mouth to devour, the darn nozzle simply bit into it, holding it firmly until she bent over to retrieve it. It took a sizable tug to release any rock so unfortunately captured.

After several minutes of practice, she was disappointed to feel Wade moving away from her. As soon as he did, it was evident why she was straddling the hose. The monster bucked and pulled like a wild mustang. Between that and the current, Jeri had all she could do just to hang on for the ride.

Wade was busying himself moving larger rocks, some so big they simply had to be rolled out of the work area. Others were picked up and thrown unceremoniously onto the rock wall. No doubt in Jeri's mind as to how that huge wall had come into existence. She was certain that each one of those rocks had been plucked from the hole they were now dredging.

After a while, Jeri became fascinated with the process. Each layer of gravel uncovered new mysteries, new beauty. It was like stripping away layers of paint, one by one, knowing that under one of those layers was an original Rembrandt. Exciting. Exhilarating. Exhausting.

Then there was a change in the floor of the creek. Instead of loose gravel wedged between layers of tightly packed rocks and boulders, it seemed to be the solid base of a single, massive water-worn rock. It had pockets and crevices filled with sand, and Jeri delighted in holding the nozzle over them, watching the gravel leap into the nozzle's waiting mouth until only the smooth, shiny surface of the rock remained.

She felt a tugging at her arm, and turned to see Wade pointing at something moving in the water. Jeri squinted at it, letting out a bubbly exclamation as she recognized three huge trout swimming toward them. The fish appeared unconcerned, circling Jeri and Wade as though they were merely the neighbors down the street, or rather, the creek.

The smallest seemed to be the most curious, and swam directly over to Jeri at mask level, hovering less than three feet from her nose as he introduced himself. Jeri could hardly contain her excitement. She dropped the nozzle, letting it fend for itself and hesitantly, slowly, she raised one hand, extending it toward the visiting fish. Warily it moved forward, finally tasting the proffered finger with a delicate nibble, then backing away quickly. Obviously, not what he had in mind.

The larger fish seemed bored with the sport, and with a quick, vibrating tail movement, called the smaller one back to the group. Then they all swam up out of the hole, and presumably, on down stream. Jeri was disappointed to see them leave, but still, it had been an incredible experience.

Petting a trout!

Then an uneasy stillness surrounded them. Something was missing...not quite right. She looked at the nozzle. It lay on its side like a dead animal. Jeri went to take a breath, and there was no air. None. My God, they were going to drown.

Wade had hold of her elbow and was propelling her toward the surface before she had time to panic. They broke the surface in a couple of seconds, both instantly spitting out the regulators and gulping air. Wade pulled his mask up, letting it sit on top of his head, and Jeri followed suit. They both looked toward the dredge. It sat quietly, floating silently on the calm surface.

"Out of gas," Wade announced. "It only goes a couple of hours on a tank full."

"We weren't down there two hours," Jeri said in astonishment. "It couldn't have been more than fifteen or twenty minutes."

Smiling indulgently, he gently guided her toward the shallows. "Being down there kind of distorts time," he said. "Seems to fly. But we're out of gas, and there you are. It's sort of the dredger's stopwatch. No gas, no air."

After they had shed the regulator harnesses, they sloshed to the bank and collapsed on the soft, grass-covered ground. Every muscle in her body trembled from exertion, and she felt totally drained. Maybe they had been down there two hours, after all. But goodness, what a glorious two hours it had been. Jeri could understand now what all the fuss was about. It didn't even matter if there was any gold in the sluice or not. All that mattered was to be down there, floating on the current, uncovering the hidden mysteries of the creek.

Finally, Jeri's muscles began to relax, and her breathing normalized. The warm air brushed her skin, a soothing, almost sensual caress, and with a sigh of complete contentment, she felt the force of gravity pull insistently at her eyelids. She was just floating into a complacent slumber when a hand covered her shoulder, shaking her gently.

"Umm?"

"Don't get too comfy," Wade told her. "We've still got work to do."

With herculean effort, Jeri pulled up one quivering eyelid. "What work?" she asked, still groggy.

"Got to clean the sluice."

"Let's leave it. It'll just get dirty again," she mumbled, turning sleepily away and curling comfortably on her side. She took another deep, relaxing breath, which turned into a muffled gasp as Wade flicked cold water on her warm back. She bolted upright and glared thunderously into his grinning face.

"Partners share," he said.

She offered a rather unladylike comment but reluctantly stood and followed him to the edge of the creek.

The dredge was tethered to a large oak growing close to the bank, and Wade used the anchor rope to pull the machine to shore. After washing the contents of the sluice into a large bucket, he showed Jeri how to screen off the larger rocks and pebbles to make the panning process easier. Then he covered a gold pan with some of the remaining concentrates and gave her a panning lesson.

"This seems easy enough," she commented.

Wade merely lifted an eyebrow and said, "Uh-huh."

Within thirty minutes, Jeri's wrist felt as though it would fall off and her hand dangled uselessly at the end of her arm. Wade took pity on her.

"I'll finish up," he told her. "You just sit on that rock and pick out the gold."

"There's not very much, is there?"

"Nope. But most of what we did today was overburden, the stuff that came down the creek with spring rains. Bedrock's where the big pieces are, stuck in pockets and crevices."

"But we hit bedrock today. I saw it."

"Yes," Wade agreed, his voice strangely quiet. "But Jerome and I cleaned that off last winter."

"Oh." Jeri watched Wade intently. His expression had gotten solemn again, almost sad. For a few hours he seemed happy and free; now something had him by the throat again, something that always seemed to take the joy from his eyes.

It was time, Jeri decided, to make her move. If he didn't tell her now, she knew instinctively that she would never find out what really happened to Jerome O'Brian.

"Isn't it cold in the winter?" she asked cautiously.

He nodded. "We use wetsuits, but it's still cold."

"Nathan and Buck told me dredging season only runs from June through September."

Wade nodded again, but didn't look up. He continued to work the gold pan deftly as he spoke. "This is a patented claim."

"What does that mean?"

"Means we own it, and can do what we want." He handed her the gold pan. All that remained was a teaspoon of black sand and dozens of tiny gold specks. He dropped a bottle in her hand. "Go for it," he said, smiling sadly.

Jeri took the pan and bottle, but instead of concentrating on her task, she was concentrating on Wade. Somehow, Jeri was intensely attuned to this man, reading every nuance of his expression, every inflection of voice. She decided to take the bull by the horns.

"Wade, what *really* happened here last winter?" she asked softly. "What happened to my father?"

A look of raw agony flickered through his eyes, his jaw clamped tightly as the corded muscles girding his strong neck vibrated with tension. He didn't look at her.

"Nothing much," he said, his tone roughened by bitterness. "I just let him die."

Jeri's breath left her in a single whoosh. She stared at Wade in disbelief, astonished not only at what he'd said, but the fact that he so obviously believed it. She opened her mouth to speak, but no sound came out.

Finally Wade straightened, tossing the still-full gold pan into a bucket with a strangled, tormented sound. His voice shook when he said, "Let's go." Abruptly, he turned away from her and started up the bank. In a flash, Jeri was by his side, tugging at his arm to pull him to a stop.

"Wait. Wade, please." She was imploring, pleading with him to talk to her. "Why... why did you say that? How could you possibly believe—"

He cut her off curtly. "It was my fault," he said. "My fault."

"How?" she whispered. "How could that be?"

Wade dropped to the ground and let his head fall into his hands. Jeri had never seen Wade so...so vulnerable, so shattered. She felt helpless to do any more than lay a comforting hand on his shoulder. After several minutes passed, she saw Wade lift his head, straighten his spine and look out over the creek.

His eyes were dull. "I guess you've got a right to know. The day he died we were working there." He pointed to the pool. "I had him moving rock while I handled the nozzle. Never should have let him move rock. Too hard. Too hard on him."

Jeri desperately wanted to say something, anything, that would help, but she followed her intuition and was silent.

Eventually Wade began to speak again, in low, clipped tones. "He signaled... he wanted to surface early. I shook him off to finish dredging that crevice—" He broke off, bitter memories etching his face with anguish. "He was sick, and I wanted to finish the damn crevice."

Wade was silent, staring sightlessly across the creek. "It was another hour before we were done. When we surfaced, he was pale, sick-looking, almost too weak to get back to the cabin. Even then, I still didn't realize how sick he was. Two hours later, he died in my arms." His eyes squeezed shut, as though to block the horror from his mind. "I just let him die. That man was like a father to me, and I just sat there, holding him, and let him die.''

Lowering his head, Wade savagely rubbed at his eyelids, as if to erase the moisture gathering rapidly behind them. Stunned, Jeri stared at him, her mind desperately trying to absorb the extent of Wade's grief and his guilt. She opened her mouth to speak, but all that came out was a strangled croak, and she took several deep breaths before trying again.

"You didn't know he was sick," Jeri told him. "I can't remember my father being sick a day in his life. If he was, he wouldn't tell anyone." She reached up and touched Wade's jaw, then tugged gently at his chin until he turned toward her. "You didn't know he had a heart condition, did you?"

He shook his head, but his expression told her it didn't make any difference.

"Well, I didn't, either. I had to hear it from Mags." Jeri's eyes had filled with hot tears that threatened to gush forward in a great, unstoppable torrent. She dashed at them furiously with her hand, gulping for control. "When he came to see me in December, he knew he only had a few months left."

Wade's head shot around. "He knew *what*?"

"I know, it doesn't make sense. I don't understand why he didn't tell me." She angrily wiped at her cheeks. "I would have come with him right away. I wouldn't have waited until..."

"I don't believe it." Wade had paled. "Mags is full of it. Jerome never would've hidden such a thing from me. We were friends, partners. He told me everything."

"Everything?" Jeri sniffed. "Not quite. He didn't tell you that he was going to bring me back to Gold Creek with him."

Wade's fingertips scoured his forehead, then he sighed. "No, he didn't, and I'll be danged if I can figure out why."

"We'll probably never know," Jeri said. "Jerome O'Brian always did what he wanted to do, lived the way he wanted to live and died the way he wanted to die." She took a deep breath and ignored the wet rush over her face. "He loved you, Wade Evans, as the son he never had. You didn't let him die. You let him live; the way he wanted to."

She was trembling, feeling Wade's pain, sharing his loss and wanting desperately to hold him against her breast, to soothe his hurt, make him whole again.

Wade reached out, wiping her wet cheeks gently with his knuckles, then pushing still-damp strands of dark hair from her forehead. "I figured you'd hate me when you found out," he said quietly. "God knows I hate myself for it."

"You know as well as I do that nobody could make Jerome O'Brian do anything or stop him from doing something he wanted to do. Daddy would be mad as the devil at you for carrying on like this."

"Yeah?" Wade's eyes were soft, and though the tears were gone he continued to stroke Jeri's face. Then his lips caressed hers in a kiss filled with sweetness and promise.

Jeri's heart constricted. She was in love.

Wearily, Jeri walked through the cabin door into the empty living room. Spending the morning with Clyde Wentz, Klamath's finest—and only—real-estate broker, had left her mentally drained and completely confused. Points, percentages, six-digit sales prices . . . Jeri was no mathematician to begin with, and the perplexing world of real estate finance totally escaped her.

No doubt, the property was perfectly suited to her needs. Not her wants, necessarily, but certainly her needs. Right off the main highway, it would give easy access to her clients, should she ever have any. The house had extremely large rooms and could easily be remodeled to contain a shop in front and living quarters in the rear. In fact, with over two

acres of land in the deal, she could even build a separate
structure for the store later on.

Naturally, the price was out of her reach. Or at least, had
been out of her reach last week. As Wade had predicted, the
down payment proved the problem. Jeri knew she could
handle the mortgage on the property but she was several
thousand short on up-front cash. It might as well have been
a million.

Now, suddenly Wentz had called her down to his office
and informed her that the down payment had suddenly
dropped within reach. The cash she had available would
make her the proud owner of two prime commercial acres
and one slightly dilapidated, four-bedroom wood-frame
house.

She should be ecstatic, but strangely all she felt was a
sense of resignation and loss along with a niggling doubt as
to why the down payment would've dropped so conve-
niently into her reach.

With a sigh, she walked into the kitchen and tossed her
purse on the table. "Wade?" No answer. Strange, she
thought. His truck was parked in its usual spot in front.

Jeri checked the rest of the cabin, then decided he was
probably in the pine thicket checking potential firewood.

Restless, she walked onto the porch and let what little
breeze there was stroke her face in an unsuccessful effort to
cool her sticky skin. She looked toward the knoll, impul-
sively calling Wade's name again. Only silence answered,
and she felt a sense of uneasiness.

Chiding herself on her foolishness, she wandered into the
meadow. Wade had always been close enough to hear her,
and she anxiously awaited his answering shout.

This is silly, she scoffed, walking faster toward the edge
of the meadow. She stood beside the vicious blackberry
bush, calling into the stand of trees beyond. Then, half
walking, half running, she backtracked and headed for the
knoll. A sense of panic dropped across her like an icy veil.

Then she heard it. From a distance, the barking of a dog. As the sound got closer, she breathed a sigh of relief. Murphy. Laughing at herself, she headed toward the sound, thankful Wade hadn't heard her screaming his name in terror. He would tease the daylights out of her if he knew she'd been worried.

The familiar yellow form appeared several hundred feet down the creek trail. Jeri walked toward him.

"Where have you been?" she called to the dog, who answered with an agitated yelp. When the animal reached her, he was barking incessantly, circling Jeri as though pursued by demons. He jumped up, paws on her shoulders and licked her face, then whined as though his doggy heart were breaking.

Dropping down, Murphy galloped back down the trail from which he'd just emerged, stopping to turn and bark at Jeri until she took a step in his direction.

The cold hand of fear gripped her throat again, its fingers closing until she could barely breathe. It wasn't her imagination. Stark terror invaded her as she sprang forward, beating her way through stinging branches and impeding brush, following the dog in a desperate, life-or-death flight.

Jeri knew it, could feel it deeply ingrained in her bones and in her heart. Wade was in trouble. Serious trouble.

Chapter Nine

Her lungs were going to burst.

Jeri's cotton slacks were shredded from falling on sharp rocks, her shirt was torn by the heedless, headlong rush through overgrown brush. She felt as though she would faint from exertion and lack of oxygen. Still she forged onward, crawling when she fell until she had the strength to pull herself up, mindlessly pushing forward, using the distant sound of Murphy's constant barking as a homing beacon.

Then she heard a new sound, a constant hum that got louder as she approached. An engine. A dredge engine.

When she reached the pool, she found exactly what she'd feared. Murphy ran back and forth at the edge of the creek, whining in an almost human show of hysteria. The dredge sat on the surface, droning and gushing. Jeri looked at it. Only water was rushing across the sluice. No rocks, no sand, no gravel. Only water. No one was guiding the nozzle.

Jeri didn't call Wade's name; she didn't have to. She knew where he was, and he couldn't hear her down there. Frantically she searched for the backpack, found it, then dug through its contents until she found her mask.

She put it on and dived into the pool.

Following the huge hose down into the depths, she headed straight toward the pit they had worked on Sunday.

Then she saw him. Thank heavens, he was moving.

She crawled toward him, using the huge rocks piled at the edge of the pit to pull herself down into the hole. Without a weight belt the surface seemed to pull at her like an invisible hand. Wade had been right about that, too.

When she reached him, she saw his leg was caught under a massive rock. He was pinned on his back, but had pulled himself into a sitting position to push at the rock. His eyes widened in surprise when he saw Jeri. Surprise turned to alarm as he pointed toward another rock teetering precariously above them. He motioned for her to surface; she shook her head.

Wade grabbed her arm and pushed her away, again pointing to the dangerously loose rock above them. Instead Jeri braced next to him and tried to push the rock away from his leg. It wouldn't budge. She pointed to the regulator and he gave it to her.

After a few gulps of air, she touched his knee, sliding her hand toward his shin caught in the rock's firm grip. The leg was cradled between smaller rocks beneath and the large one above. One wrong move and the large rock would instantly crush his leg. The only way was to move that boulder.

And Jeri was determined to do just that. Somehow.

Quickly she surfaced, searching desperately through the stash of shovels and other tools until she found what she needed. Grasping a five-foot pry bar and a large shovel, she jumped back into the pool, sinking quickly under the weight of the tools.

First she positioned the shovel's wide blade part way under the rock and motioned for Wade to reach up and grasp the handle. He pulled himself into a sitting position and grabbed it, then held the mouthpiece toward Jeri. She sucked a quick breath before maneuvering the pry bar as far as possible under the other side of the rock. If they could only raise it an inch, Wade's leg would be released from its rocky prison.

Laying the bar flat, she pushed it as far as it would go under the rock. She looked at Wade and saw that he knew exactly what they had to do. He pulled down on the shovel handle with all his strength, and the rock vibrated. At the same moment, Jeri braced herself with her feet against the massive piece of granite and pulled up on the pry bar.

With every ounce of strength available to her, Jeri squeezed her eyes shut and pulled up on that bar. Its sharp edges cut into her hands, her arms felt as though they were being pulled from their sockets, and behind her locked eyelids explosions of light blinded her brain.

Then she felt nothing at all.

When she opened her eyes, Wade was carrying her to the bank. Murphy circled them both, rollicking and splashing through the shallows with exuberant relief at the return of his humans.

Wade lay Jeri gently on the grass. "Little fool," he murmured. "You could've been killed."

Groggy at first, Jeri blinked up at Wade, disoriented, wondering why he was leaning over her, chest bared and dripping, with such a grim expression. Then the crisis flashed back in her mind, vivid color images of their desperate struggle beneath the deceptively calm surface of the dredge pool. Her eyes widened as memories of the terrifying experience gripped her.

"Are you all right? Your leg..." Jeri's gaze went to Wade's knee. Hesitantly, she reached out as he knelt over her and feathered her fingertips over his calf. Wade responded to her touch with a slight quiver.

"My leg's fine. Just a bruise." His forehead furrowed in what could have been considered a fierce scowl, if not for the expression of concern softening his eyes. "You're a dang fool for going down there." His voice broke slightly, and the stern reprimand didn't quite come off.

"I wouldn't leave you," she said, eyes wide with shock that he could even consider the possibility. "Why did you go down there alone? You told me it was dangerous. Why did you do it?"

Her voice vacillated from pleading to scolding to exasperated frustration, and Wade appeared embarrassed to have been caught doing exactly what he'd warned her never to do.

Hesitantly, he met her eyes, then gave her a tentative, rather self-conscious smile. "I never said I was particularly smart." He looked sheepish. "Always did give orders better than I took them."

A sputtering noise turned their attention toward the dredge. The engine hacked once before it coughed into total silence. They stared at it with bloodless faces. Both of them knew Wade had been mere minutes from certain death.

Propping herself on one elbow, Jeri stared at the monstrous machine floating like a bloated log on the pond. A combination of sheer terror and uncontrollable rage tore at her innards. That horrible metal beast, that blasphemous, ugly collage of hose and steel, had nearly killed Wade. The thought overwhelmed her.

Reaching up, her hand trembling uncontrollably, Jeri touched her palm to Wade's face. "I can't lose you, not now. If anything ever happened to you..." She couldn't verbalize the unthinkable.

"I'm all right, honey." His voice shook. "We're both all right."

Their eyes locked. "Are we?" she whispered, and saw her own mental turmoil reflected in his expression. "Are we all right, Wade?'' Her index finger traced a shaky line from the side of his brow down to the sharply angled cheekbones and continued lightly along the contours of the molded hollows beneath.

He didn't answer her poignant question, but when the tip of her finger paused at the corner of his mouth, Wade grasped her wrist. He brushed his lips across her palm, then held it tightly against his cheek. ''Sweet thing,'' he said finally, ''I haven't been all right since the day you walked into my life.''

His gaze raked her body, the flaps of fabric torn from her shirt hanging wet and dripping against her body, while bloodied welts were revealed on the soft skin beneath. He wanted to scoop her into his arms and soothe her pain. His heart felt as though it was being squeezed in a vice. What was happening to him?

''Wade?'' Her voice was a husky whisper. She sat up, her eyes locked to his darkening gaze, and slipped her free hand up the broad expanse of his chest. Dropping her wrist, Wade reached out, and she launched herself against him, throwing her arms around his neck, burying her face in the roughened skin of his throat as her sobs shattered the serene silence.

Murphy circled them anxiously, whining with concern as Wade and Jeri sat locked together, rocking in rhythm like branches arcing against the wind. Since the immediate crisis had been resolved, the dog appeared confused by the continuing emotional display. Finally, Murphy sauntered down the bank to rest in a patch of sun.

Wade held Jeri until her body stopped its violent shuddering and her involuntary sobs had given way to an occasional shivering hiccup.

''I'm sorry.'' She sniffed and wiped at her eyes. ''I'm not usually so overwrought.''

The sweet, fresh scent of her assaulted Wade's senses. He buried his face in the curve of her neck, deeply inhaling her fragrance.

"You feel so good in my arms," he said. "Soft and fragile. A perfect fit."

He slid one hand up to tangle in her wet hair while pressing the other against the small of her back, massaging with slow, circular motions while holding her even more tightly against his bare chest. Her low, throaty whimper vibrated against his neck, sending an army of goose bumps marching in formation across his spine.

He shuddered, and Jeri locked her arms tighter as she felt the spasm traverse the length of his body. Hesitantly, she pressed moist, parted lips to his neck, tasting him. Shocked at her own boldness, she withdrew, continuing only in response to Wade's whispered encouragement. Soon instinct won over inexperience.

She wanted to absorb him, taste him until his flavor permeated her completely. It was as though Jeri had been a pot of bland broth, waiting only for the right seasonings and enough heat to simmer to a glorious, pungent soup.

Wade's entire body went rigid as he felt her lips against his throat. He felt her hesitation. The awkwardness of her movement was a forceful reminder of her innocence, her inexperience. His breath caught, then slid out in a long, low sigh.

With herculean effort, he pulled his hand from her back and, reaching behind his neck, he loosened Jeri's grip. His other hand was still tangled in her hair, and he gently pulled her head back, moaning with regret as her warm lips left the sanctuary of his flesh. "Jeri . . . honey, no."

Jeri seemed bereft at the loss. "What's wrong with me?" she asked softly. "Why do you push me away?"

Wade gently lifted a damp strand of hair from Jeri's flushed cheek, then slid the back of his hand lightly across her face in a soft, shaky caress. "There's nothing in the world wrong with you, Jeri. You're special, very special."

And young, Wade reminded himself. Too young.

He'd been fighting himself since the moment he'd seen her, wanting her in a way he couldn't quite comprehend, yet knowing he had a duty to protect her. Still, there was something different about this woman and the mental torment he was going through because of her.

Wade felt her tremble against him, vulnerable, trusting. She'd risked her life for him, and he was humbled by her courage and her selflessness.

So many years he'd been isolating himself. Isolation may not have been the best way of life, but it had been less painful than disillusionment and loss.

If you give your heart to a woman, she'll eventually crush it and laugh while you bleed, Wade thought sadly. Yet a small voice in the corner of his mind seemed to whisper insistently that this was different. *Jeri* was different.

Wade desperately wanted to believe that voice.

"Checkmate." Ben Hawkins pushed his shiny black bishop into position on the chessboard, then leaned back in his chair. "Either I'm becoming a world-class player, Wade, or you've been sitting there with your head in a dark place for the past three weeks."

Wade blinked across the table as though awaking from a deep sleep. "Umm? What'd you say, Ben?"

"I said 'checkmate'... same thing I've been saying every night since your new partner showed up." Ben scratched his stubbly chin, eyeing Wade's bleak expression. "Anything you want to talk about?"

Wade ignored Ben's question. "It just proves that I'm a good chess teacher. Got any more beer?" Wade got up and went to the refrigerator, opened the door and stared inside. Ben had been right. Wade's thoughts hadn't been on chess, tonight or any night since Jeri O'Brian had walked into his life. He'd done everything he could to get her out of his house, out of his life. Now that she was going, he felt empty, as though one of his vital organs had been surgically removed.

"If you're trying to commit suicide, it'd been a hell of a lot quicker in the oven," Ben said.

Wade straightened and scowled at him.

Undaunted, Ben droned on. "'Course, it's a sight more original, holding your head in the fridge until your brain freezes, but it takes too long and you're using up all my propane."

Wade grabbed a cold beer and threw it toward Ben with more force than necessary. With a deft movement, Ben snagged the can and popped the tab. "Not that I blame you," he said, then took a quick swig. "Sweet little thing like that comes waltzin' in, wiggling her assets, it's enough to drive a man to drink."

The refrigerator door slammed, and Wade spun around. "Watch your mouth." Wade's voice was deadly. "She's Jerome's daughter."

"So? She's still a woman and a fine-looking one at that." Ben's eyes sparkled through his impassive expression. "Have you sampled the merchandise?"

Wade reached out, grabbed Ben's shirt and yanked him to his feet. "Don't you ever, and I mean *ever*, talk about Jeri like that again."

A knowing smile crept across Ben's face. "You seem a mite touchy tonight."

Wade's fingers uncoiled like tightly-wound springs, and Ben stumbled backward. Mumbling an apology, Wade dropped into his chair and stared at the scattered chess pieces.

Repositioning his own chair, Ben settled into it and took another swallow of beer. "How long have you been in love with her?"

Wade's eyes narrowed, then closed. He sighed. "I don't even know what love is, Ben. I thought I did—twice." Callused fingertips scoured his eyelids. "I don't know what's wrong with me. I've never felt like this before."

"Umm."

Wade's eyes flew open. "What the devil does *that* mean?"

Ben shrugged. "Keep your socks on. Caring about somebody ain't something to be ashamed of. Lord knows, I loved my Gladys." A soft light flickered in his eyes, then died sadly. "How I miss that woman."

Not knowing what to say or how to comfort his friend, Wade simply nodded. It had been three years since Ben's wife had died, and Wade knew he still grieved for her. It's frightening, Wade thought, to allow another person to have that kind of control over your heart and your mind. He'd known Jeri was dangerous to his sanity the first time he'd laid eyes on her. Blast it all, he'd tried to be careful, to keep himself from weakening. But careful wasn't enough with O'Brian's daughter. She had a hold on his heart and his mind that was different than anything he'd ever experienced. It scared the hell out of him.

Ben sniffed once, blinked, then looked at Wade as though he'd just materialized. "So." Ben covered the break in his voice with a cough. "So, what're you gonna do about her?"

Shaking his head, Wade spoke slowly, as though each word was an effort. "It's already done. She's going to leave."

"She's giving up her share?"

"No, but she's moving out. She's buying the old Barnes place."

"That broken-down hut? What on earth for?"

Wade smiled. "She's going to open an art shop."

"You're putting me on."

"Nope. She says the valley needs culture." Wade's laugh was dry and tight. "That's probably my fault. I took her to Happy Jack's."

Ben stared at Wade as though he'd lost his mind. "Even *I* don't go to Happy Jack's."

"Me, neither." Wade had the grace to look sheepish. "I thought it'd scare her away."

"Since she's still here, I guess it didn't."

He winced. "She handles herself better than you'd think."

"I believe it," Ben said solemnly. "She got right puffy about you paying for her car."

"Umm. She's got a thing about taking anything from anybody. I guess she's trying to prove that she's not like her mama." Wade's expression sobered. "She'll go off like a rocket if she finds out that I paid half her down payment so she could have that darn art store."

"Why'd you do that?" Ben sounded exasperated. "You know dang well you don't want her to leave."

"Because it's something she wants, Ben, something she's wanted all along." Sighing, Wade raked at his hair. "I've got no right to stop her."

"No, but you didn't have to help her, either." Ben looked skeptical. "How'd you do it, anyway?"

"I made a deal with Clyde Wentz. I paid half the down payment, and he told Jeri that the owner dropped the price."

"'Course, you gave Clyde a little something for his trouble." Ben's disapproval was obvious. "Must be nice to have that kind of cash just lying around."

Wade winced. "It wasn't exactly lying around. I was going to pay property taxes with it."

With a disgusted snort, Ben shook his head. "You're flat-out nuts."

"Maybe."

"So how're you gonna' handle those taxes?"

"I've called in a couple of bonds, but it'll take a few days to cash them out."

Ben's breath whooshed out in a long, telling whistle. "That'll cost a bundle."

"A few bucks in penalties." Wade knew he sounded too defensive. "I can handle it."

"Yeah," Ben said. "Sure." His crooked fingers drummed the table before he pronounced, "I think you'd better marry that woman while you've got a shred of good sense left."

"Marry?" Wade's eyelids snapped to attention, then narrowed. "I don't think you've been listening to me, Ben. She's got what she wants."

"Maybe not." Ben pursed his lips. "Maybe there's something else she wants."

"Yeah," Wade said. "She wants Gold Creek."

The painting was completed. Jeri stood back, looking at the image she'd created, swallowing the lump in her throat. This painting was for Wade and, in many ways, for herself, as well. No gallery would ever show it. Captured on canvas was the true essence of her father's life through one of his greatest loves—the creek itself. Jeri had realized that by giving her Gold Creek, Jerome had actually bestowed so much more. In that one legacy, her father had left her a sense of who he was and, in return, who *she* was.

At Gold Creek, Jeri had come to terms with herself.

Jeri thought again of her mother, of the sad, empty shell of a woman she'd become, never allowing herself to love or even to care for another human being. Not even for Jeri.

Was protecting herself from possible pain worth the certainty of a cold and loveless life? The question battered the final shards of her emotional defense. A few months, a few weeks, whatever fate granted her with Wade, she decided to take. She opened herself, accepting her love for him even as she had accepted the man himself.

If she couldn't hold the wind, Jeri told herself, she could at least feel its soft touch caress her as it passed.

Deep inside, Jeri still refused to accept that loving Wade was completely hopeless; the painting portrayed her desperate faith. She would, after all, still be in the valley. Just a few miles away, in fact. And half of Gold Creek still belonged to her, and always would. Wade would have to see her. It would just take a little time, a little patience. But Jeri knew—simply had to believe—that eventually Wade Evans would come to her with love. He just had to.

Carefully draping the still-wet canvas, Jeri took it to her room and tucked it out of sight. It was nearly lunchtime. Maybe Wade would be back soon.

She went to the kitchen and cleared the table, smiling at the ever-present paper clutter. It seemed he was always spreading reams of it across the table and poking on his tiny calculator as though pondering the fate of some giant corporation.

Normally she simply stacked the scattered folders in a neat pile, but today she idly leafed through them. Deeds, legal papers, bills. Normal stuff, but each sheet had Wade's imprint, his aura, and she handled them lovingly.

Something caught her eye. Her father's name was written on one document, partially buried in the stack. She freed the paper and quickly scrutinized the contents. A document from the county tax assessor to Wade Evans and Jerome O'Brian as co-owners, listing parcel and lot numbers and survey land descriptions meaning less than nothing to Jeri. She already knew the parcel in question was Gold Creek.

She read the sheet, sucking in her breath sharply. This was not simply a tax bill. This was denial of a requested extension to pay. Thumbing through the stack, Jeri was stunned to find half a dozen identical letters; only the parcel numbers and lot descriptions were changed. They all said the same thing: *Extension of payment deadline denied.*

Obviously, someone had made a mistake. A big one.

Jeri grabbed the telephone, quickly punching out the number listed on the letter.

The feminine voice on the line was annoyingly cheerful. "County tax assessor's office," she chirped. After explaining her problem, Jeri listened with increasing frustration to a maddening selection of elevator music as one person after another pushed the Hold button.

Finally, Jeri got ahold of a Bob Taylor and summed up her problem. "Obviously, there has been a mistake," she said.

A pause. "No mistake, miss. The full amount was due and payable last month. There's a grace period, of course, but the taxes will become delinquent at the end of the week."

"Delinquent? Good grief, what will happen to the property?" Her fingers whitened on the receiver. Mags had implied that Wade was having financial troubles, but Jeri had never even suspected that it could be this bad.

"Well, eventually it would be sold, of course. The county has a duty to its taxpayers to foreclose on delinquent property—"

"How can you do that? How can you just take someone's property and sell it off?" She realized that she sounded like a hysteric, but at the moment, she was feeling somewhat hysterical. If Wade lost his property—lost Gold Creek—it would destroy him.

Bob Taylor sounded indignant. "We don't just 'sell it off.' It would be auctioned, fair and square, all perfectly legal."

"When?" she squeaked. "How long before you could do that?"

"Well, it would probably take a month or two, if it came to that."

"Oh, no." Heavily, Jeri dropped her body into the nearest chair. The letters represented thousands of dollars in taxes due on all of Wade's properties. What would happen to Mags and the Blackthorns and all his other tenants? Would they be turned out and left homeless?

That's exactly what would happen, she knew with a certainty. Cold chills skittered down Jeri's spine.

Jeri couldn't let that happen. But how could she help? How could she possibly...? Of course. She could use her down-payment money.

Her voice was calmer now. "Keep those papers handy, Mr. Taylor. I'll be there in an hour." She dropped the receiver back into its cradle.

Naturally, Jeri would have to stay at Gold Creek a bit longer. Wade wouldn't like that, but he certainly couldn't refuse and leave all those people out in the cold.

She smiled.

Chapter Ten

Nervously smoothing the flared skirt of her best, and lowest-cut, dress, Jeri posed in front of a full-length mirror. The silky, cream-colored fabric accentuated her golden tan, clinging curvaceously to waist and hip while the plunging neckline revealed a tantalizing hint of ivory swells beneath.

She brushed her thick hair until it shone like a cap of fine Siberian sable and carefully applied mascara to thicken her lashes into a heavy dark fringe. A quick dab of light pink lip gloss and the deed was done.

Jeri studied the results and pronounced them disappointing. She dumped her meager stash of cosmetics onto the bed, rifling through them as though searching for an overlooked tube of instant miracle. No such luck. She did discover her only bottle of cologne and gave herself a couple of quick squirts, hesitating only slightly before adding another spray between her breasts.

"One can only hope," she murmured. This might turn out to be her last opportunity to make Wade see her as a woman. Wistfully, she wondered what it would be like to make love with Wade, to feel his arms around her and pretend that he cherished her, cared for her, even for a little while. After all, when he found out what she'd done, he might just toss her out on her ear.

Reaching deep into her purse, she pulled out the tax receipts and slipped them into a manila folder. Wade wouldn't be happy about this, she knew. He would be embarrassed that she'd discovered his financial problems and furious when he found out that she'd paid his taxes. Men were so pigheaded about these things, she thought, but Wade's offended ego would be more than appeased when she gave him the quitclaim deed.

Lightly fingering the official-looking document, duly notarized and stamped by the county recorder, Jeri had a spasm of pain. "Please understand why I have to do this, Daddy," she whispered. "You loved him, too." She slipped the deed into the folder with the tax receipts. Gold Creek belonged to Wade now, all of it, nice and legal.

Opening the bedroom door, she went into the kitchen to turn the marinating steaks. Jeri stared at the beautifully set table, then promptly rearranged the utensils. Everything had to be perfect tonight, absolutely perfect. She chewed at her lower lip and mentally rehearsed the evening she'd planned. First, she would ply him with his favorite foods, champagne, mood music—the whole nine yards. Then, when he was well-fed and relaxed, she would say, "Wade, I know how broke you are, so I used my entire savings to pay your taxes."

Moaning aloud, she gave the salad a halfhearted toss and anxiously glanced at the clock. It was getting late. He should be here soon, and she had absolutely no idea how she was going to tell him without sounding like some kind of idiot. Jeri could only hope that Wade's anger would dissipate when he saw the deed and realized that Gold Creek belonged totally to him.

The telephone rang, exploding Jeri's taut nerves. She jumped a foot and shredded lettuce flew into the air, floating to the shiny floor like stringy green confetti. Again the phone jangled loudly, and Jeri answered it breathlessly.

There was a hesitant pause, then a male voice said, "Who's this?" When she answered the question, she heard a sharp intake of breath. "Let me talk to Wade," the voice said sharply.

Taken aback by his rudeness, Jeri stammered, "He's not here. I can have him call you—" Click. He'd hung up on her. The nerve. She was still fuming when Wade's truck drove up in front of the cabin, turning her anger to ice. Nervously, she began to bustle around the kitchen, picking up the scattered bits of lettuce and preparing the steaks for broiling. The cabin door opened.

"Hungry?" she called cheerfully. Wade loomed in the doorway of the kitchen. Murphy, not to be denied a closer sniff, pushed by Wade's lean leg and bounced into the room. He stood at Jeri's feet, panting happily, tail wagging in anticipation of some special culinary delight. Jeri smiled at the dog, then looked toward the doorway. Her heart caught in her throat. Wade was so incredibly handsome. For a moment, she wondered what she would do if Wade told her to leave. He could now, she knew. After all, the quitclaim had been officially recorded. Jeri was no longer his partner.

Of course, he didn't know that yet.

Still, Jeri had to look away. If she thought about leaving the valley, leaving Wade, she would get all teary-eyed and drip mascara on the meat. Almost savagely, she shoved a fork in one steak and flung it on the broiler. Jeri could almost feel Wade's eyebrow raise. She forced her voice to be light and cheerful.

"I thought a celebration was in order," she said. "So I planned a special dinner."

"It's not my birthday, so you must be celebrating your new art store." His voice left no doubt that he wasn't in a party mood.

Jeri stiffened. "Well, sort of."

Wade made a muffled sound and issued a tense nod. Jeri frowned briefly, wondering why he seemed so somber. After all, he still thought she'd bought the property and would be leaving. That should make him ecstatic.

"Beer?" she asked, smiling brightly.

He shook his head curtly and sort of grunted. Jeri's lips pursed in puzzlement. No beer. Maybe he's ill. That would sure put a crimp in her plans.

Wade jammed his hands in the pockets of his jeans and skulked into the center of the kitchen. Leaning against the counter a few feet from where Jeri was working, he glanced from the candles on the kitchen table to the large, juicy steaks being arranged on the broiler.

"Looks like quite a celebration," he said. "Who else is coming?"

Surprised, Jeri looked up. "No one. Why?" She followed his gaze down to the three steaks and laughed. "This is a celebration for all of us," she said, and looked down at Murphy, who positively quivered in anticipation.

In spite of Jeri's efforts, dinner was a tense affair. Wade was sullen and withdrawn, his conversation limited to an occasional responding mutter. Normally voracious, his appetite seemed more appropriate for an anorexic teenager than a strapping woodsman as he merely poked at his plate before pushing it away. He left the kitchen without a word, leaving Jeri hurt and disappointed.

From the doorway, she watched Wade drop wearily onto the sofa, squeezing his aching forehead, as though attempting to exorcise some demonic force.

He seemed so sad, she thought, and wondered why. She hesitated briefly, then went into the living room to implement phase two of her plan.

When he saw her, Wade straightened, replacing his anguished expression with an impassive stare. Slowly, she walked to the sofa to stand in front of him and held out two partially filled glasses.

"What's that?" His voice was gruff as he eyed the amber liquid with obvious disdain.

"Peach brandy," Jeri said. "It's supposed to be quite good." She favored Wade with her most dazzling, sexiest smile, but he didn't respond. Obviously, her inexperience showed, she thought wryly. But determination should count for something, and Jeri was certainly determined. Lowering her eyes demurely, she batted her lashes once in a rather blatant Scarlett O'Hara imitation. Wade stared at her bleakly.

"Champagne, brandy. Heck of a housewarming," he observed grimly.

Wade leaned stiffly against the soft leather sofa cushions holding the brandy glass as though it were a coiled snake. He watched her vacantly as she sat next to him, allowing her arm to brush his shoulder. Smiling, she clinked the rim of her glass against his and laughed, a low, throaty sound. Like Bette Davis.

"It's not poisoned," she said, then slowly, seductively raised the glass to her lips. Her eyes were dark and inviting, peering over the crystal rim to lock with Wade's penetrating stare.

The golden fluid inched toward her lips, then flowed into her mouth in a boiling stream of molten lava, searing her throat and settling in a hot mass in the pit of her stomach. Her entire body revolted against the vile intrusion, and with a violent spasm, rejected the evil liquid.

Jeri's eyes widened in shock when the brandy took over, spraying across her lap as a fit of coughing left her helplessly convulsed.

Wade yanked the glass from her hand and began to pound mercilessly between her shoulder blades. Finally, Jeri caught her breath. Wiping her watery eyes, she looked at the sticky mess covering her lovely dress, then up at Wade. His mouth twitched. Jeri felt her face flame with humiliation.

Wade set both glasses firmly on the coffee table. "I guess you'd best stick to wine coolers," he said, the comment flustering her further.

She wondered if it was possible to salvage the romantic mood she had so diligently tried to create. "I guess you're right." Jeri managed a smile. "It's just that this might be our last evening together, and I was trying to make it...uh, special."

"Last evening?" Wade stiffened. "You're just going two miles down the road."

"Well, that was the plan, of course, but..." Not now. She didn't want to get into this now. Jeri wanted to see that soft, heated glow return to his eyes. Her voice was a husky whisper. "That's two miles farther away than I am right now." Then she parted her lips provocatively and leaned forward just enough to offer him an enticing view of her cleavage, such as it was. But she was desperate to make him see her, want her.

What she received for her effort was a stunned expression that quickly turned to one of acute annoyance. "What in the world is wrong with you, woman?" he demanded. "First you try to kill yourself by chug-a-lugging hundred proof, now you act like you're already sopped." He cocked an eyebrow suspiciously. "Have you been snorting cooking sherry?"

Oh, good grief. Nothing was ever easy.

But she had started this, and she was going to finish it. Jeri was feeling desperate. This could be her last chance to show Wade that she loved him. Maybe she'd come to mean more to Wade than he wanted to admit, too.

It was time to commit herself. She wouldn't even consider the humiliating possibility of failure. Tonight she needed to create a memory, perhaps the last memory, with the man she knew she would spend her life loving. Tonight was hers, and she decided to go for it.

Standing quickly before she lost her nerve, she reached behind her back, unzipping her dress and letting it fall in a filmy puddle around her feet. She stood before him, wearing only a silky slip and a terrified expression.

It was several long seconds before Wade appeared to regain control of his limbs. Shock and disbelief flared through his eyes like neon, and his mouth dropped open, jaw dangling like a door with a broken hinge.

Jeri stood rigid, motionless, silhouetted in the mellow shadow cast by the room's softly diffused illumination, her body glowing in the amber light like a porcelain statue.

Suddenly, the reality of her ludicrous situation dawned on her. She, who was perhaps the only twenty-five-year-old virgin in the entire state, was trying to seduce an unwilling man. Some unearthly entity must have taken possession of her body, Jeri thought wildly. A strange demonic force must have simply fried her brain cells, and in a convulsive fit, her hand had flailed out of control. No sane person would rip her own clothes off to get a man's attention. Demonic possession was the only explanation. She would simply explain to Wade that she'd suddenly been struck brain-dead. Yes, that's exactly what she would tell him. As soon as she could move her mouth.

Wade managed to rehinge his jaw and was clearing his throat to make certain his vocal cords still functioned. His voice was rather like a strangled gurgle when he said, "Trying to tell me something?"

Blinking rapidly, Jeri was certain she saw a flicker of amusement flare briefly in the blue-green depths. Then his mouth twitched.

Oh, No. He's laughing at me.

And why not, she thought miserably. Certainly the sight of a grown woman parading through his living room wearing only underwear and goose bumps could be considered rather humorous.

"I'm . . . not very good at this," she lamented, hating the croaky quaver in her voice.

Cocking one eyebrow, Wade hooked his thumbs in his jeans as though to keep his hands under control, then took a couple of unhurried steps toward her.

"I dunno," he drawled. His gaze traveled the length of her, slow, deliberate and appreciative. "Looks pretty good to me."

Skin that had chilled to frost point began to thaw and steam under the heat of his blazing scrutiny. Mesmerized, Jeri was fascinated by his eyes, darkened until only a thin circle of color ringed huge pupils. They seemed to bore into her very soul.

Standing in front of her now, he was so close she could feel the heat of his body, see the dark curling hairs peeking from the neck opening of his shirt. Her palms itched to touch him.

His voice was low, husky. "Honey, my conscience and me, we've been doing battle since the day I laid eyes on you, and I'm getting tired of fighting it." He released his thumbs from their looped prisons and rigidly dropped his arms to his sides.

Jeri's gaze was riveted on the top button of his shirt. To her shock, two unidentified hands appeared in front of her face and began to fumble at his buttons. The alien hands with the inept, numb fingers seemed to be attached to her arms, and they struggled valiantly until the shirt fell open.

With a sigh of contentment as her palms met hair-roughened muscle, she traced the hard contours with electrified fingers. She felt rather than heard the groan rise from beneath her palms to catch in the sinewy cords of his throat.

Then Wade's hands were on her, encircling her body, splaying against the curve of her spine, mesmerizing the feel of rounded hips, touching her everywhere at once and setting a blazing trail of flame from breast to navel and below. His lips were at her throat, tasting its softness before moving to capture her earlobe in a bone-chilling caress.

"You're so beautiful," he mumbled hoarsely, cherishing her with his eyes, absorbing her beauty as a dying man absorbs hope. "I think old Ben has the right idea."

"Umm, Ben? What idea is that?"

"He said I should m—" He sucked at her throat, drowning the words against her soft skin.

With the piercing wail of the telephone, Wade felt Jeri stiffen.

"Don't answer it," she whispered. "Please." She gripped his shoulders, as though she feared that if he left her then, he'd never return.

Wade's lips brushed her throat. "It might be important, honey." His smile was slow and seductive. "Don't go away."

The telephone continued its insistent screams, and Wade forced himself to release Jeri. He strode impatiently across the room and barked into the receiver.

A vaguely familiar male voice greeted him. "Wade? This is Harry Landsing, from the mill."

"Harry? Haven't seen you in months. What's up?"

Harry sounded nervous. "Well, I know this isn't any of my business, Wade, but..." He paused.

"Spit it out, Harry. I don't have all night." Wade slanted a glance at Jeri, relaxing slightly to see that she hadn't come to her senses and run out of the room.

"Well, hell, Wade. I just thought you ought to know, that's all."

"Know what? Harry, what's this all about?"

"I was down at the tax assessor's office this afternoon talking with Bob Taylor. You remember Bob, don't you? His wife, Sarah, always brings that noodle pie to the mining council potlucks. Well, Bob gets this call while I was there."

Wade impatiently rubbed at his eyes. "Can I get back to you, Harry? I'm kind of busy right now."

"It was her, Jerome's daughter."

That got Wade's attention. "What did she want?"

Harry sounded uncomfortable. "That's the part I thought you should know. She was asking all kinds of questions about what would happen to your property if you didn't pay the taxes on time."

Wade's voice could have etched cold steel. "Are you sure about that?"

"Yeah, I heard the whole thing. Bob was telling her about how it'd be auctioned off and everything, and she wanted to know exactly when that would happen." Harry paused to let Wade absorb that astounding bit of news. "It sounded to me like she was planning on being the first one in the bid line."

Wade's eyes hardened into cold, gray stones, a muscle in his jaw twitching as his mouth stretched into a taut line. He'd been right. She was only after the land. The woman he'd thought himself in love with was coldly calculating how to get Gold Creek all to herself. It hurt.

"Wade?" Harry's voice sounded like a distant hum. "Are you there . . . ?"

Wade dropped the receiver softly into its cradle.

Jeri was staring at him, eyes wide with shock and concern. "What is it?" she asked softly. "What's wrong?" She took a step toward him then froze, as though something in his expression had impaled her.

Wade's jaw was clamped so tightly that his teeth ached, and his voice sounded raspy, hollow. "I hear you've been making some phone calls."

Confusion flickered briefly across her face, then Wade saw her eyes widen. It's true, he realized bitterly. All of it is true.

Her hand went to her throat. "I—I didn't mean to pry. The letters were on the table, and I saw them," she said quietly, amazed that her voice could echo such quiet strength while her heart was pushing on her tonsils. "I called the tax office to see what I could do—"

"Do?" Wade's voice burst through the room like a bomb. "To get your hands on my property?"

"What? No, of course not..." Her voice trailed off. "I'd planned to tell you about it tonight."

Wade's face was dark with anger, but he wasn't looking at Jeri. He stood rigid, a shadowed silhouette carved from ebony granite, and suffered the awakening of long-repressed anguish. In his mind's eye he saw Denise's flowing strands of flame-colored hair and ice-blue eyes filled with ridicule, scorning his love, mocking him. Wade was caught in a time warp, mentally suspended in the past, consumed by his own suppressed fury.

He'd been fooled again.

Shakily, Jeri scooped up the dress puddled at her feet. "I can see that you're upset," she whispered, clutching the material to her chest as trembling fingers twisted it into a silken spear. "I'd hoped that you'd understand."

"Oh, I understand all right," he said, with a dry, unpleasant laugh. "*You're* the one that's got things all screwed up. There isn't going to be any auction." He felt pain rather than satisfaction as her face paled. "I've got the money."

"But the letters... Mr. Taylor even said that the taxes were already delinquent." She shook her head, totally confused. "If you had the money, why didn't you just pay them?"

"That's none of your business."

Her shoulders squared. "As co-owner of Gold Creek, I happen to think it *is* my business." Sheer stubbornness kept her from mentioning that she was no longer a co-owner. Jeri managed to keep her chin steady. "I did what was necessary to protect my property."

"That's one way to put it." Wade turned his back toward her as he rebuttoned his shirt. His shoulders were stiff.

"Wade, please listen," she said. "I had no idea you'd be so angry. I care about Gold Creek and I…care about you." Her voice softened to a whisper. "I mean, we've come to mean…a lot to each other, and I didn't really want to leave. Maybe we can work things out if—"

"*If* what?" Wade spun, grimacing. It was a manipulative ploy, he told himself. She's negotiating, trying to trade herself, her body, for the land. "If I give you what you want, then I can have what you're offering?" His gaze raked over her as she trembled before him, ineffectually trying to cover herself with the wad of silky material. "Your daddy would be real proud if he could see you right now."

"No…" she whispered, the sound a vague, almost inaudible moan. "It's not true. Please…don't make it sound ugly."

"No thanks, honey, the price is too high, and I've paid enough already."

"I—I don't understand."

He made an unpleasant sound. "You didn't really think the price on that property you wanted for an art store just dropped on its own, did you?"

Every ounce of blood seemed to drain from her body. Jeri's eyes widened, staring out from her pale face like pennies trapped in a snowbank. "The down payment—you paid the difference." She stared at him, eyes shimmering beneath a thin sheet of unshed tears. "Why?"

Wade clenched and unclenched his fists, powerful biceps flexing under the strain. *Why?* he thought. Because it had been something she'd wanted, and Wade would have handed her the moon on a string if she'd asked for it. He had wanted to see the light in her eyes, the happiness on her face.

And because he was in love with her.

The anger drained from him, replaced by an expression of pure desolation. "How else could I get rid of you," he said, then turned and walked into the night.

* * *

All shred of illusion was gone now.

Jeri knew that the soft expression in Wade's eyes when he'd looked at her was pity, nothing more. Her world may have exploded when he touched her, but his hadn't. Anything else she wanted to believe was pure fabrication, the futile hallucinations of a woman in love.

As dawn's gray pall filtered into the kitchen, Jeri placed the manila folder containing the tax receipts and quitclaim deed on the table. Wade would be certain to find them there.

"Wade." The whispered name rolled from her tongue. Look what she'd done to him. She'd forced herself on him, made him so desperate that he'd risked financial ruin to get away from her. Time and time again he'd tried to tell her, but she wouldn't listen, had been blind to the truth. He really didn't want her, never had, never would.

Pain and frustration overwhelmed her. Wade's accusations were vile, cruel and humiliatingly true. She cringed at the memory. An offering of total love and complete commitment had somehow been turned into a shameful charade.

Now it was over. Her suitcase was packed, and it was time to go. Perhaps she should write a note, some light and airy little line about keeping in touch, but she just stared at the blank paper until the edges seemed to undulate and blur beneath her unblinking gaze.

There was really nothing left to say. The look of contempt on Wade's face last night haunted Jeri. He'd stared at her with absolute loathing, as if the mere sight of her had made his skin crawl.

Pushing the paper away, she picked up her suitcase and walked to her car. Jeri took nothing she hadn't arrived with except four neatly-bound stacks of letters.

And a broken heart.

Chapter Eleven

Wade stared at the wrinkled paper strewed across the kitchen and muttered another explicit oath. When he'd realized Jeri had paid the taxes on Gold Creek out of her own pocket, he'd crumpled the receipts savagely and flung them across the room.

He stared blackly at the quitclaim deed, absorbing its taunting message before a vicious backhanded swipe sent the document sailing across the room to bounce off Murphy's flank. The startled animal beat a hasty, judicious retreat into the relative safety of the living room.

Wade couldn't believe it, but there it was, a quitclaim signing Jeri's half of Gold Creek over to him. The official-looking time stamp taunted him. Yesterday morning. First she'd transferred her half of Gold Creek to him, then she'd paid his taxes. Last night.... Wade cringed at the thought. Last night was to have been a celebration of her gift to him, the gift he'd thrown back in her face with lies and accusations. Guilt and pain gnawed at him.

Why couldn't he have simply accepted that it was possible for something pure and beautiful to become part of his life?

The telephone rang, and Wade snatched the receiver from its cradle, barking angrily into the mouthpiece.

"Don't you go snapping at me, Wade Evans," Mags said. "Now, where's Jeri? She didn't show up for my lesson this morning."

"Gone." It was a hoarse croak.

"Gone? Gone where?"

"Just gone." Wade was instantly defensive. "Back where she belongs. It was about time she came to her senses."

"That so?" replied Mags testily. "When're you going to come to yours?"

Wade grunted.

"You're dang stubborn, Wade Evans," Mags said. "Go on and keep your pride, since it's so all-fired important to you, but I can tell you right now you'll end up a lonely, bitter old man without even a sweet memory to keep your wrinkled feet warm at night."

"This isn't your affair." Wade was sullen and hurt. "Besides, it was her choice. I didn't throw her out—exactly."

Mags muttered some uncharitable comments under her breath. "And just what—exactly—did you do?"

There was a long silence while Wade rubbed at his forehead.

How else could I get rid of you?

His own words haunted him as he stared at the crumpled quitclaim deed. "You don't want to know," he said wearily. "And I don't want to talk about it."

"Good Lord, boy!" Mags said in exasperation. "That woman's in love with you, and I wouldn't mind betting my egg money you're just as sweet on her. Now go find her."

"I can't, Mags. It's too late."

He dropped the telephone receiver softly back into its cradle.

Haggard from a sleepless night, Wade was unshaven and as rumpled as the hapless receipts scattered around the room. His mind reeled, under siege by a deluge of contradiction and confusion. He'd all but convinced himself during the grueling predawn hours that he was better off without her, that she was no different than the other women who'd wreaked havoc on his life. Selfish, manipulative and greedy, every one of them.

Wade had known his heart would never be free of Jeri O'Brian, but perhaps his mind would survive. After all, he'd told himself, she was just like the rest of them; just like Denise.

Then these ominous sheets of paper shredded his carefully woven fabric of self-delusion. A selfish woman doesn't use her own money to pay someone else's bills without thought of reward, and a greedy one wouldn't give away two hundred thousand dollars' worth of property.

Fool woman. Stubborn, just like her daddy.

Wade's thoughts drifted to Jerome O'Brian. Wade knew that his old partner had been aware that his health was deteriorating and had deliberately sought out Jeri to bring her back to Gold Creek—and to Wade. The ornery Irishman had known all along that Wade and Jeri belonged together, but Wade had been too pigheaded to acknowledge it.

Now he'd lost her.

As though pulled by an invisible cord fastened to his solar plexus, Wade was drawn toward Jeri's room. He stood beside the bed, which was tidily made and as neat as the day she'd first appeared in his life. Picking up the fat pillow, he buried his face in it, deeply inhaling the sweet scent of her.

Still holding the pillow against his chest, he walked to the closet and pulled the door open, half hoping to see some forgotten garments that would announce her imminent return.

There was nothing, except . . .

Wade's gaze was drawn to a strange, darkened shape propped in the shadows. Reaching to touch it, he felt its roughened terry-cloth covering and, dropping the pillow, used both hands to lift the towel-covered painting from its secret place. He set it on the dressing table, propping it securely against the wall.

His breathing shallowed, and his hands shook as he reached out to remove the cloth. When he uncovered the painting, his heart lodged behind his Adam's apple and nearly choked him.

On that canvas, Jeri had captured the spirit, the very essence of Jerome O'Brian's love for the land.

Soft shades of green and saffron shaped the familiar beauty of the creek knoll. The sky was a clear, cornflower blue, yet a huge mass of puffy white clouds billowed above the horizon.

There was something subtly different about those clouds, something that drew the eye. Softly veiled by color and stroke, the muted contour of a face with twinkling blue eyes and approving smile could be seen, almost lost in an outline of whitened beard, which again became the surging cloud mass.

At that moment, Wade knew exactly how dear Gold Creek was to Jeri and just how much it had cost her to give it up.

A fiery sun clung low on the midday sky, almost blinding Jeri as she urged her car around the final hairpin curve toward Mags's house. The vehicle clunked and jerked, sputtering to a stop as it heaved across the driveway.

Out of gas. Wonderful.

Exhausted and mentally drained, Jeri wrapped her arms around the steering wheel and rested her face against the hard plastic. The chill against her cheek was a soothing contrast to the heat of her fevered skin. She should be halfway to Redding by now, and Jeri cursed the hours she'd spent driving around the valley or simply sitting by the river. She'd been saying goodbye to the Klamath. Now she'd say goodbye to Mags.

The pain and frustration were overwhelming. Jeri remembered her painting. The painting—that very special expression of her most personal feelings—had been left behind, carefully tucked in the back of a closet. She'd intended to give it to Wade, but now realized that he wouldn't want it. It would only remind him of a time she knew he wished only to forget.

The painting would only be special to her, Jeri realized. Maybe someday she would find the courage to write him and ask for its return.

Someday, she thought miserably.

"Jeri? Lord, child, is that you?" Mags stood on the porch and blinked.

Jeri managed a smile and climbed out of the car. "Hi, Mags. I know I'm late for our lesson."

Wiping her hands on her apron, Mags headed down the porch steps. "Never mind the lesson. You just tell Mags what's wrong."

Jeri hoped her bright smile was convincing. "Nothing's wrong."

Mags's shrewd gaze skimmed to the back seat of the car. "Why's that suitcase in there?"

"Because the trunk is full." As though to prove her point, Jeri went to the rear of the car and opened the trunk. Easels and canvases were stuffed between two bags of paint supplies. Jeri handed one of the bags to Mags and shoved a couple of blank canvases in the woman's free hand. "How about some of your famous iced tea?" Jeri lifted the last sack from the trunk and the two women carried the parcels into Mags's kitchen.

Mags peeked into a bag. "Goodness, child. Looks like you bought out the hobby shop."

"Not quite." Jeri retrieved a small canvas that had slipped from her grasp and bounced across the kitchen floor. The warm, spicy scent of something wonderful permeated the cozy room. Jeri sniffed appreciatively.

Mags grinned. "Cinnamon rolls," she said. "Near ready. Don't suppose you'd care to test one?"

Jeri's stomach rumbled, as though to remind her that she hadn't eaten since yesterday. "Twist my arm."

"Now what's all this?" Mags waved her hand at the cluttered table.

On that cue, Jeri reached into the first sack and pulled out a handful of brushes, several tubes of oil paint, turpentine, paint thinner and a flat wooden palette.

"It occurred to me that you'll need to practice your art between lessons." A bright smile. "Supplies."

A gray eyebrow lifted in surprise, then lowered as Mags shrewdly scrutinized first the art supplies, then Jeri's smiling face. Mags's lips pursed. "Don't know as how you could call what I do 'art.' At least not yet." Mags fingered a tube of paint. "This is all new. Where'd it come from?"

Jeri avoided Mags's knowing gaze and busied herself by emptying the sacks. "I went to Yreka this morning."

With a swift, decisive motion, Mags pushed the paint tube away. "This cost a pretty penny, and you're going to be needing it for your store. Lord knows I'll be your best customer, even if I'm not your most talented student."

Jeri's face remained impassive as she rummaged through the second bag. She was unsettled by Mags's intense, questioning gaze but managed to keep her voice cheerful. "You've got plenty of talent, Mags, but you won't develop it unless you practice." Out of the sack came two books on painting technique. "Use these. They're the most helpful of their type." Jeri set the books on the table amid the tubes and brushes.

Mags picked up one of the books, flipped idly through it then fixed Jeri with an intense stare. "I talked to Wade a bit ago. He's a mite upset."

Jeri stiffened. "I've made a mess of your kitchen." She scooped the clutter back into the bags. "I'll just set these on the counter, out of your way."

"He said you'd gone. Seemed to think you was leaving the valley."

Jeri busied herself straightening canvases and ignored Mags's conversation. "Now, you're going to have to set aside at least two hours a day for practice. Follow the lesson plan in book one."

Finally, Mags sighed. "You've a good heart, Jeri O'Brian, and I thank you for the gifts."

Jeri fiddled with a sable brush, fanning the soft hairs across her palm, unable to meet Mags's eyes. "You've been a good friend, Mags. I—" The thought seemed to choke her. "I came to say goodbye."

They stood in silence, an awkward, palpable hush of quiet gloom that chilled the warm fragrance of the room.

"Jeri..."

"I need a favor, Mags." Words rushed out. "I ran out of gas. Silly, isn't it? Well, there you are. I just wasn't paying any attention and—"

Mags saw the sheen of tears and enveloped Jeri in a motherly embrace. "There, there, child. Mags will take care of everything. You just sit right down and have one of these fine cinnamon rolls."

Before Mags busied herself at the oven, Jeri noted a strange, smug look on the woman's face. A warning alarm buzzed in Jeri's brain. "Mags? Don't you dare call Wade."

Mags appeared offended. "Why, I wouldn't!"

But the smug expression remained.

Good grief. What time was it?

Startled, Jeri awoke and saw shadows slanting across Mags's guest bedroom. Obviously, Jeri's momentary rest had turned into a major nap. She rubbed at her eyes. They burned. Another reason to avoid tears, she told herself.

So much for mooning self-pity. Even if she dreamed of Wade Evans every night for the rest of her life, Jeri was determined she wouldn't turn into a vegetable.

The man didn't want her, for heaven's sake. There was nothing to do but get on with her life. She would be darned if Wade or any other man was going to turn her into a whining, sniveling drip.

"Do you hear that, Wade?" she mumbled softly. "You can just take a flying leap into your dredge pool. I don't need you."

Jeri knew it was a lie. Part of her would need him forever, want him forever. Love him forever.

She shook off the thought, ran her fingers through her hair to comb it and stumbled into the living room. It was quiet. Jeri wondered if Mags had any luck borrowing a can of gas from one of the neighbors. A quick inspection of the kitchen proved fruitless. No Mags.

Then Jeri heard a rumbling sound, like a truck engine revving. She glanced out the window in time to see her battered yellow car disappear down the road dangling from Ben Hawkins's tow truck.

"Hey!" She flung herself out the back door. "Come back here." A swirl of dust and fluttering leaves answered her command. Her breath whooshed out. "He took my car. He *stole* my car. Mags!"

Jeri ran to the edge of the driveway and stared down the empty road. A familiar blue truck was roaring toward her. Jeri's jaw sagged as Wade pulled to a stop beside her. Murphy barked joyfully, leaping from the truck as Wade opened the door. The dog circled Jeri, panting and grinning, until Jeri gave his sleek head a stiff pat. Once acknowledged,

Murphy trotted into the shade and stretched out to watch the proceedings.

Wade tried to smile, but the effort failed dismally. "Hi."

He saw Jeri's eyes darken in anger and noted the tense set of her jaw as she glowered at him. Not that he blamed her for being mad, of course. He'd behaved like a fool, and that was a fact. Bless Mags, though. She'd called Ben, Ben had called Wade, and now Wade had every intention of convincing Jeri that Gold Creek was her home.

At the moment, however, Wade saw that he had a bit of a problem. Jeri was, to say the least, not happy to see him.

"You've got a nerve," Jeri whispered angrily as her heart hammered against her ribs. She did a smart about-face and walked stiffly toward Mags's house.

In two strides Wade was beside her, slipping his large hand around her elbow. "Come on, honey," he said. "Get in the truck."

His eyes locked with hers, and he felt a sharp pain penetrate from his chest to his navel. Her fragile face mirrored pain and outrage, and it tore at him to know he'd caused it.

Clamping her jaw stiffly, Jeri drew herself up to full height, and when her chin was even with the middle of his chest, she threw her head back and stared him right in the eye.

"Flake off," she said.

Wade frowned down at her. "I'm not leaving without you."

"Then you can just sit here until you grow roots. I'm not going anywhere with you. Ever."

Trying to ignore the warm pressure of his hand on her arm, she gave her elbow a yank. He yanked back, and she bounced off his chest.

Panting and trembling, her eyes darted toward the narrow road, as though searching for escape. Wade caught the movement and captured her wrist. She stared down at the invading hand.

"I saw the painting," Wade said.

Her body went rigid. "You had no right. It was... personal."

"You meant me to see it. That's why you left it."

"It was an accident. I forgot it. I want it back."

"Come up and get it." Wade's voice was like rough silk, caressing her senses until her skin seemed electrified.

"No." She pulled vainly against his manacled grasp.

"Jeri." His tone was urgent. "I don't blame you for being angry, but we've got to talk."

"I don't want to talk. And I *want* to be angry. I'm *enjoying* my anger." She gave him a sinister stare.

"You're sick," Wade mumbled, a smile playing at the corner of his mouth. "But I still want you."

"Well, I don't want you," she lied, her voice rising to an almost hysterical pitch. "Why in the world would I continue to fling myself at a man who keeps throwing me back like an undersized trout."

Wade cocked his head, the half smile still dancing at the corner of his lips. "Want to ride in front, or do I have to hog-tie you to the roof like a deer?"

Lifting herself on the balls of her feet, Jeri thrust up a defiant chin, infuriated by Wade's amused expression.

"Read my lips, Wade—*go away*." In sharp, biting tones, Jeri accentuated each word with the shape of her mouth. Wade's gaze seemed glued to her lips.

"Read mine," he murmured, giving her hostage wrist a quick pull until she fell stiffly against his chest, then encircling her with his arms until she was effectively locked against him. He fitted his mouth over hers, gently moving his lips against hers as he felt her body stiffen, unyielding as she pushed feebly at his chest. On a small, desperate gasp, her lips parted, and his tongue slipped into the dark softness, probing and caressing as her small frame melted fluidly against the hard muscles of his body.

At last, slim arms wrapped around his neck, pulling him down to her as he swallowed her small, sweet whimpers. Reluctantly, he ended the kiss, looking deeply into her wide eyes clouded with confusion and desire.

"We have to talk." He ignored the husky tremor of his voice.

Jeri nodded mutely, allowing Wade to lead her to Mags's porch. From his vantage point, Murphy seemed to recognize that the crisis was over. The dog bounded to the porch, and Jeri braced herself for the assault. Murphy's paws hit her shoulders at the same time his wet tongue swiped a juicy path across her face.

"Mind your manners, Murph," Wade admonished, though not in a particularly stern voice.

The dog circled them, barking with excitement while Jeri wiped the remnants of Murphy's kiss from her face with the back of her hand. She smiled at him, and the dog lifted his muzzle, staring up with total adoration.

Wade and Jeri sat on the wooden porch step, casting nervous, furtive glances at each other. Jeri drew strange, irregular shapes in the soft dirt with a long stick; Wade tensely crushed a dry leaf into coarse bits.

Finally Jeri cleared her throat. "You wanted to talk."

Wade nodded. "Yeah."

"Well?"

"Huh? Oh, well, I've ... um ... been thinking." Silence extended for several, painful moments before Wade spoke again. "What I did...I mean, the things I said..." He sighed in exasperation. "Good God, honey," he exclaimed, flinging the leaf dust into the muggy air. "I was wrong."

Jeri's eyes widened. "Of course, you were wrong."

"Yeah, well..." Wade scoured his head until his hair stuck out in thick brown tufts. Reaching up, Jeri automatically smoothed it for him. He caught her hand and held it to his lips. "I'm a fool."

"That's true."

"When Harry told me you were pumping the tax office about auctioning land for delinquent taxes, I thought..." He shrugged helplessly.

Jeri's lips pursed. "You just automatically assumed the worst about me, like you've been doing since the first day I arrived."

Wade looked sheepish. "Mags says I'm a pigheaded jerk."

"Mags is right."

He winced. She wasn't making this a bit easy. "I didn't mean what I said to you, honey. I never paid that down payment to get rid of you. I didn't want you to leave."

"You certainly fooled me." A thought struck her. "Where did you get the money, Wade? Mags says you don't get enough rent from your tenants to keep a flea alive."

"I still own a couple of business parks outside of Sacramento." He mumbled at the ground. "And a small high-rise in San Francisco."

"A *small* high rise?"

He grinned. "Only ten stories, but the office space is always filled."

Jeri was stunned. Wade was casually describing real estate worth millions. "I can imagine."

"The rent from those properties and interest on a few bonds lets me live comfortably."

"Then why couldn't you pay your taxes?"

A frustrated sigh. "I never said I couldn't pay them. You said that."

"Now, wait a minute. I saw the delinquent notices—"

He held up a hand to stop her. "I just needed a couple of extra weeks to liquidate some bonds."

Jeri was beginning to grasp the overall picture. "You'd already used the cash you'd set aside for taxes to pay my down payment."

"I wanted you to be happy, that's all. I thought that art store would make you happy, so..." His voice trailed off, and he skimmed a look toward Jeri. She was chewing her lower lip.

"Why didn't you tell me, Wade? It was a kind, generous thing to do. Why did you hide it?"

"Because you're stubborn, that's why. Because every time someone does something for you, you throw it back in their face."

Jeri's mouth tightened, and her eyes glassed with hot mist. He was absolutely right. When Wade had tried to pay for her car repair, she'd acted as though he'd insulted her. "I do get a bit pompous, don't I?"

He agreed with a grin. "And I get a bit bad-tempered, mean-mouthed and mush-brained, but that's all behind us now." Then he sobered. "Jeri... honey... let's go back now," he said.

Jeri just bent her head lower, shaking it from side to side. "No," she said. "I invaded your home once, and look at the mess I made of it. There's sure no reason to do it again."

"There's one."

Cautiously, she looked up. "What's that?"

His mouth twitched, and now it was Wade's turn to flick nervously at the dusty ground. He cleared his throat, then coughed nervously and cleared his throat again.

"Wade?" Jeri's voice was becoming impatient, as though steeled for another zinger and anxious to get it over with. "Give me one good reason why I should go back to Gold Creek?"

"Because I love you," he mumbled, his voice so low she barely heard him speak at all.

It was the hardest thing he'd ever done, saying that. It was like unzipping his chest to expose his pulsing core so she could reach right in and pluck his heart out. A look, a word, could shatter him as he sat before her, totally vulnerable, helpless and humbled by the powerful surge of emotion swelling his chest.

"What? What did you say?" Jeri's voice was incredulous.

In a burst of courage, Wade's head snapped up and he looked her straight in the eye. "I said I love you." Loud and clear.

Jeri just stared, unable to believe what her ears were relaying. "You can't. You... you don't know how," she finally blurted.

Wade's jaw dropped, and he gaped at her.

Jeri's mouth was open, stunned at the verbal heresy that had spilled from her own lips.

Suddenly, Wade burst into a fit of laughter. "Danged if you aren't half right, honey. I *didn't* know how." Bending toward her, he encircled her waist in his arms and hauled her onto his lap. "I sure did learn, though. You're a heck of a teacher."

He kissed her, a deep kiss, both passionate and tender, giving and demanding, as his body trembled with the force of his newly acknowledged love. All that mattered at this moment was the woman he loved beyond reason, the woman who'd completed his soul when she suddenly appeared in his life and gave it meaning—a purpose.

"Honey," he whispered against her pliant lips, "I *do* love you. I know I'm not any prize, but I promise to spend the rest of my life trying to make you happy. I want to marry you, if you'll have me."

Jeri tangled her fingers in his thick hair. "Oh, I'll have you," she whispered. "You're an ornery, oversized son of a grizzly, but I love you, too."

Their lips met, holding, moving together as though starved for the taste of each other. When the kiss ended, Jeri stroked Wade's whisker-roughened jaw, smiling at the uncharacteristic stubble.

"But you already knew that, didn't you?" Jeri asked softly.

Wade's eyes shone, darkened to a rich, blue green. He gently stroked her cheek with a callused fingertip, then trailed it down the curve of her jaw and length of her smooth throat until it rested in the pulsing hollow. "Do you think you can spend the rest of your life as the wife of an ornery, oversized son of a grizzly?"

"Of course, I can. I'm stubborn, just like my daddy."

Epilogue

Jeri tucked the inventory sheet onto her clipboard and rearranged the tallied items on the shelf. "I'm worried sick. In the year Wade and I have been married, Murphy's never done anything like this."

Mags looked up from the display of brushes she was counting. "He didn't come home at *all* last night?"

"No. He'd been so restless the past couple of days, then he just took off. I wanted to search the far side of the creek, but..." Jeri rubbed at her back and glanced at her bulging tummy.

"Not in your condition." Mags pursed her lips. "Why don't you go on home. You're looking a bit peaked. I can lock up."

Jeri smiled. Mags was not only her best friend, the wiley woman had become Jeri's partner in the Evans Art Mart. Wistfully, Jeri remembered the thrill of opening the art shop that had been her dream. Wade had been so proud, and the art store's success had soared beyond Jeri's wildest dreams.

Such a wonderful year, topped by the small miracle she now carried under her heart and, in a few weeks, would carry in her arms. Wade's child, her child. If only her father could have shared her happiness....

A jangling bell captured Jeri's attention. She and Mags turned to see Wade blasting through the front door of the shop. Jeri's face lit with joy as she ran into his arms.

"Easy, honey." Wade's palm rested protectively on her swollen tummy. His lips brushed her forehead. "I found him."

"You found Murphy? Is he all right? Oh, thank heavens." She sagged briefly against his chest, then stiffened. "Where is he? Are you sure he's not hurt?"

"He's just fine, honey, just fine." Wade frowned. "You're getting all upset, and it's not good for you. It's not good for the little one, either."

"You're such a worrywart. We're both just fine."

Wade didn't look convinced and noted Jeri's hand massaging her back. He moved his own palm into place, warming and kneading her tense muscles. "Why don't you let Mags run things for a while, honey. You work too hard."

"Umm. I'm fine. I love to work."

Wade sniffed the air. "Paint fumes," he pronounced. "Turpentine and paint fumes. It's not good for you."

"The ventilating system you installed does a fine job of cleaning the air. Considering the fact that it cost more than the property itself, it should." She gave his nose a playful tweak. "What you smell, Mr. Evans, is the disinfectant air purifier you insisted upon. We are both—" She patted her tummy for emphasis "—perfectly healthy."

"Well..."

"Why didn't you bring Murphy with you?" Jeri's smile died. "Where *is* he?"

Wade grinned. "Come on, and I'll show you."

Mags agreed to lock up the store, and Wade helped Jeri out to the truck. Jeri accepted Wade's solicitous nature with amusement and resignation as he lifted her, setting her gently on the newly-cushioned truck seat.

Two months ago, Wade had decided that the vibration of the hard truck bench was dangerous for Jeri and the baby. Wade had wanted to buy a plush, luxury sedan. Sweet of him, Jeri realized, but a totally impractical vehicle for the dirt roads of the valley. They had compromised by re-upholstering the truck cab in soft squishy padding. Including the dashboard . . . and the doors . . . and the roof . . .

Once Jeri had buckled herself into both of the special seat belts Wade had installed for Jeri and her growing tummy, they headed down the highway. Wade was tight-lipped about Murphy's mysterious whereabouts, and Jeri was about to burst with curiosity.

She was even more confused when Wade pulled into Ben's Gas Station and parked.

"This is it," he said cheerfully, then loped around the truck to lift Jeri out. Ben leaned out of a doorway, greeted them, then motioned them inside.

Bewildered, Jeri allowed Wade to propel her into Ben's small office. She gasped.

In the far corner was Ben's dog, Lulu, laying on a pile of shredded newspaper. Lulu looked tired, and judging by the number of squirming puppies wobbling over her legs, she had every right to be pooped. Murphy sat beside the wriggling brood, panting happily, looking enormously pleased with himself. The big Lab yipped a pleasant greeting.

"Oh, they're beautiful." Jeri dropped to her knees for a closer look. Some of the puppies were long-eared and liver-colored like their mother, some were spotted with white, and some were bright yellow. Not much doubt of parentage here.

"I found them all out back under the big cottonwood," Ben said. "Feel kind of foolish, though. I just thought she was getting a bit fat."

Lulu gave her master a disgusted look, and Jeri laughed. "May I?" Jeri motioned to a fat, yellow puppy, then scooped it up when Lulu consented by licking Jeri's hand. "Oh, Wade. It looks just like Murphy."

Wade agreed. Murphy's chest seemed to puff.

The puppy was round and warm, its blunt nose wiggling as it sniffed the strange human scent of Jeri's hand. Eyes squinched tightly, the puppy's head wobbled, then the pup's mouth clamped onto Jeri's thumb and gummed it noisily.

"I'd say that pup just claimed you," Ben said.

Jeri looked up hopefully.

Wade cleared his throat and tried to look serious. "Well, I guess there's enough room up at the creek for another set of paws."

Smiling, Jeri rubbed her cheek against the puppy's soft fur. "Just one?" On cue, Murphy muzzled a fat brown ball out of the wriggling mass.

Wade sighed. He could scowl and argue, but it would just be for show. There was nothing in the world he wouldn't do for his wife, and everyone in the valley knew it.

Soon, a child's laughter would echo across Gold Creek meadow. O'Brian's dream was alive, and his legacy of love had finally been fulfilled.

Jerome would have been pleased.

*   *   *   *   *

Silhouette Romance®

LONG, TALL TEXANS

Diana Palmer brings you the second Award of Excellence title

SUTTON'S WAY

In Diana Palmer's bestselling Long, Tall Texans trilogy, you had a mesmerizing glimpse of Quinn Sutton—a mean, lean Wyoming wildcat of a man, with a disposition to match.

Now, in September, Quinn's back with a story of his own. Set in the Wyoming wilderness, he learns a few things about women from snowbound beauty Amanda Callaway—and a lot more about love.

He's a Texan at heart . . . who soon has a Wyoming wedding in mind!

The Award of Excellence is given to one specially selected title per month. Spend September discovering *Sutton's Way* #670 . . . only in Silhouette Romance.

RS670-1R

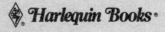
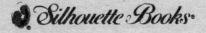